"I want you to marry me, Cory. I want our son to have a proper father."

Cory winced. "I've already told you I won't marry you."

Struggling for calmness, Slade said, "Don't you think it's time you started to figure out all the implications of what you're saying? There are three people involved here, not just you. And one of them is our son."

"I should have drawn up a contract for our agreement. Instead, I trusted your word. Big mistake," Cory retorted.

Only the sure knowledge that he was fighting for his life enabled Slade to keep his temper. "I want to live with you, Cory. For the rest of my days."

Although born in England, *SANDRA FIELD* has lived most of her life in Canada; she says the silence and emptiness of the north speaks to her particularly. While she enjoys traveling, and passing on her sense of a new place, she often chooses to write about the city which is now her home. Sandra says, "I write out of my experience. I have learned that love with its joys and its pains is all-important. I hope this knowledge enriches my writing, and touches a chord in you, the reader."

Books by Sandra Field

HARLEQUIN PRESENTS
1739—THE SUN AT MIDNIGHT
1762—THE DATING GAME
1806—BEYOND REACH*
1830—SECOND HONEYMOON*
1862—AFTER HOURS*
1919—UNTOUCHED
1964—GIRL TROUBLE

*Significant Others trilogy

Don't miss any of our special offers. Write to us at the following address for information on our newest releases.

Harlequin Reader Service
U.S.: 3010 Walden Ave., P.O. Box 1325, Buffalo, NY 14269
Canadian: P.O. Box 609, Fort Erie, Ont. L2A 5X3

SANDRA FIELD

Honeymoon for Three

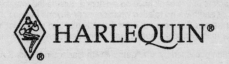

HARLEQUIN®

TORONTO • NEW YORK • LONDON
AMSTERDAM • PARIS • SYDNEY • HAMBURG
STOCKHOLM • ATHENS • TOKYO • MILAN • MADRID
PRAGUE • WARSAW • BUDAPEST • AUCKLAND

ISBN 0-373-11982-8

HONEYMOON FOR THREE

First North American Publication 1998.

Copyright © 1996 by Sandra Field.

This edition published by arrangement with Harlequin Books S.A.

Printed in U.S.A.

CHAPTER ONE

SLADE REDDEN ran his eye down the day's list of appointments. "Cory Haines? Who's he? Another politician looking for a handout? If so, he's clean out of luck."

Mrs. Minglewood coughed discreetly. "Cory Haines is a woman, Mr. Redden. She owns a landscape design company here in the city."

"And what does *she* want?"

"She did not disclose the nature of her business, sir. But she was quite insistent that she have an appointment as soon as possible."

She'd want something. Everyone did these days; it was one of the penalties of success—or so Slade was learning. Ever since he'd won that international award for his inner city design in Chicago, realtors and bureaucrats and architects had been after him in droves. He rubbed his eyes. He hadn't slept well last night, and the mixture of rain and snow that was choking the air was no incentive to get to work. Halifax, capital city of Nova Scotia, one of Canada's eastern seaboard provinces, had obviously not heard of the concept that March was supposed to usher in the season called spring.

Mrs. Minglewood regarded him sympathetically. She liked working for Mr. Redden on his rare visits to the company offices in Halifax; he was, in general, even-tempered, and treated her as though she was a real person and not a piece of modular furniture. Hidden somewhere in her capacious bosom was the added factor that he was easily the most attractive—not even in her secret

5

thoughts would Mrs. Minglewood use the word sexy—
man she had ever laid eyes on. None of the heroes of
the old movies she doted on could compare with him.
They didn't even come close.

"...at lunch?"

Flustered, she said, "I beg your pardon, sir?"

Patiently Slade repeated his question, and within half
an hour Mrs. Minglewood had enough work to keep her
busy the whole day. But she was not so busy around two
o'clock that she didn't watch for the arrival of Cory
Haines.

At three minutes to two the elevator doors opened and
a young woman stepped out. She approached Mrs.
Minglewood's desk and said in a pleasantly low-pitched
voice, "I have an appointment with Mr. Redden at two—
my name is Haines."

Mrs. Minglewood's bosom indulged in a pleasurable
flutter of romanticism. Without a speck of envy—for
she loved her stout, garrulous husband Wilfred and considered herself a truly happy woman—she decided that
Cory Haines was exactly what Mr. Redden needed on
such a miserable day. A real pick-me-up. "Come this
way, please," she said, and tapped on Mr. Redden's door.

Slade had been absorbed in the computer printouts of
one of his latest projects—a renewal of the harbor
frontage. He wasn't happy with the placement of the
boardwalk, but he couldn't quite put his finger on what
was wrong. "Come in," he called brusquely. He'd give
this appointment ten minutes. Maximum.

Cory heard the brusqueness and squared her
shoulders. He wouldn't be the first business executive
to give her grief, nor would he be the last. Although his
CV hadn't led her to expect real problems.

"Ms. Cory Haines, Mr. Redden," Mrs. Minglewood
said, and hesitated just a fraction too long before re-
gretfully closing the office door.

Cory walked into the office as though totally confident of her welcome. The magazine articles she'd searched out had prepared her for Slade Redden's rugged good looks. But in person the man was far more impressive than any two-dimensional photograph could possibly portray. Oh, my goodness, she thought. It's a good thing I'm immune...talk about an unfair advantage.

Slade, quite unjustly, had pictured a gray-haired martinet with a jutting chin. He saw a woman considerably younger than his thirty-four years who nevertheless possessed that indefinable something called presence. In an attractive contralto voice she said, "It's very good of you to spare me some of your time, Mr. Redden. I know how busy you are."

He stood up automatically, wishing he'd taken the trouble to comb his hair. His tie was askew, his jacket draped over the chair and his shirtsleeves rolled up. Oh, well, she'd have to take him as he was.

At six feet he topped her by three or four inches. "May I take your coat?" he asked.

It was a smart navy blue trenchcoat. As she slid it from her shoulders, he caught the scent of her perfume, a subtle blend that hinted of warmer climates; the overhead lighting caught in her smoothly groomed hair so that it gleamed like strands of copper. "Please sit down," he said, hanging up her coat, pushing the papers on his wide mahogany desk to one side and getting right to the point; he rarely wasted time on social niceties. "What can I do for you?"

He watched her take a moment to gather her thoughts. Her flared wool skirt, kingfisher-blue, worn with a richly embroidered vest and a white silk shirt, spoke of a woman confident of her own taste, who took pleasure in texture and colour. Her face, he thought, rather surprised both at his interest and his acumen, was like a good painting; something to which you could return again and again, always with reward. She was excited about something, he thought slowly. Very excited.

Cory leaned forward in her chair and smiled at him, a smile that warmed her dark brown eyes. Just because he was easily the most attractive man she'd ever met, she saw no reason to change her game plan. "I want something from you, Mr. Redden—and I'm willing to give you something in return."

"Then you've just differentiated yourself from a great many people who come through that door," he said drily.

"Have I?" Her lashes flickered. "You're a very successful businessman—but I think you really care about the quality of your work and how it affects those who live with it. And that, I'd say, differentiates *you* from a great many people."

She'd neatly turned the tables on him. "And why do you believe that about me, Ms. Haines?" he said, then wondered if she'd think he was fishing for compliments.

"I've done my research—I've read everything I could find about you and your company." Again her inner excitement welled up, causing her words to tumble out. "You and I have something in common, I'm convinced of it—and it's on the basis of that certainty that I'm here. Because if your time is valuable, so also is mine."

She wasn't being arrogant; she was simply stating a fact. Intrigued in spite of himself, Slade said, "You have an advantage over me. Because I know nothing whatsoever about you."

"I own my own company too: Haines Landscaping." Her lips quirked. "A much smaller company than yours. I've been doing landscape design in this area for five years, and last year I won both a municipal and a provincial award for a community park I designed in the north end of the city."

Unable to contain her energy, she got up, walking over to the tall windows, which were streaked with rain, and gazing down into the street. "I love this city, Mr. Redden. I want it to be a good place for people to live. I want it to stay human-oriented...user-friendly, if you like. And that's where you can help. Because I think you share those values."

"I'm not averse to making money," he said sharply.

"Neither am I. Nor do I apologize for that."

He leaned back in his chair, linking his hands behind his neck, feeling the pull on his chest muscles. "So what kind of a touch are you going to put on my checkbook?"

A flush rose in her cheeks. She jammed her hands in the pockets of her skirt and said with noticeable coolness, "I don't want your money. I want your land."

She was nothing if not straightforward, thought Slade. For some reason wanting to jolt her out of her composure, he said, "Land is money—surely I don't have to spell that out for you?"

"Land is a lot more than money. *I* don't have to spell that out for *you*." She bit her lip, leaving a trace of peach-toned lipstick on one tooth. "Specifically, I'm interested in two properties—the old parking lot on Dow Street, and the corner lot on Cornell and Cruikshank. Neither one is what you'd call a desirable property in monetary terms."

He got up too, and walked over to the window, his gaze trained on her face. "So why do you want them?"

She said with an intensity he was almost sure she was unaware of, "The parking lot on Dow Street could be made into a wonderful community garden—plots for individual families, small sheds for equipment, a shaded playground at the far end for the children whose parents are working in the garden. As it is now, it's a wasteland—garbage all over the place, potholes, nothing to please the eye. Or the soul."

Deliberately needling her, Slade said, "How very eloquent of you."

Cory looked straight at him, her eyes narrowing. She might want something from Slade Redden but that didn't mean she had to let him walk all over her. "Am I standing here making a fool of myself?" she said. "All those magazine articles that spoke in such glowing terms of your integrity and your old-fashioned values—were they just exercises in fiction and flattery?"

In a leisurely fashion that stopped just short of insult, Slade let his eyes wander over her face. Her lashes were thick and dark, and many a model would have paid a fortune to have her cheekbones. Quelling a crazy impulse to wipe the tiny fleck of lipstick from her tooth, and thereby feel the soft curves of her lips beneath his fingertip, he said abruptly, "What about the other property? On Cornell?"

"There are a couple of old people's homes near that corner, as well as some low-rental housing. It could be made into a small park with benches, flowerbeds and shrubs—there are already three fine maples there for shade."

"You design it and I pay—is that the deal?"

Her nostrils flared. "There's no need to be gratuitously offensive, Mr. Redden."

"You can always leave," he said evenly.

"And then kick myself for the next month because I gave up too easily? No, thanks!"

He was only confirming what he already knew. "You really do want these projects to go ahead, don't you?"

"Of course I do," she snapped. "I wouldn't be here otherwise—I already told you my time is valuable."

"So what would your contribution be?"

"If you donated the properties to the city on the condition that they be kept as a garden and as a park respectively, I'd provide the design, the plants and the labor.''

He raised his brow. "That's exceedingly generous of you... What's your motive, Ms. Haines?"

She said pleasantly, "It's been a long time since I've met a man who riled me as much as you do. Could my motive possibly be altruism? Or won't that wash?"

She hadn't left his office and she hadn't backed down. "Nope," he said. "Altruism, in my opinion, doesn't exist."

"I would consider that statement arguable." Her smile was consciously provocative. "How about enlightened self-interest? Are you more susceptible to that?"

"You're getting closer."

"I'm a quick learner. As for my motive, I get the pleasure of seeing worthless land made both beautiful and useful. How will that do?"

"It's going to cost you."

"I can afford it."

"I hadn't realized landscape design was so profitable."

For the first time he saw that he'd got beneath her skin. "The source of my money is none of your business," she said shortly. "I can afford it. That's all you need to know."

"I'd need documentation to that effect before making any commitments."

"You'll have it." She swallowed, feeling tension tighten her jaw. "Are you saying you'll consider my proposal?"

"I'm free tomorrow morning between ten and eleven-thirty—that should be enough time to check the sites out."

"I have an appointment at nine. I could pick you up outside your office at ten-thirty."

I have a life too; that was what she was saying. He grinned at her. "I'll be there. Bring your plans."

"Thank you," she said blandly. "Let me give you my business card in case there's any change in the time." Stooping by her chair, she extracted a neat green and beige card and passed it to him. Making no attempt to hide the sardonic note in her voice, she added, "It's been a pleasure meeting you, Mr. Redden."

"Likewise, Ms. Haines," Slade said, and took her coat from the hook, holding it for her. Her hair was pulled into a knot at her nape, long hair the colour of polished chestnuts; again her scent drifted to his nostrils. It was a long time since he'd been so aware of a woman, so awake to every tiny detail... a very long time.

Quickly Cory shrugged into her coat, not wanting to prolong the contact of his hands on her shoulders. She turned to face him. "I'll see you tomorrow," she said.

Suddenly resenting her level gaze, Slade said, "I'm sure you'll understand that I'll be running a routine check on your business between now and then."

"I wouldn't expect otherwise."

Irritated out of all proportion, he swung the door open. Mrs. Minglewood looked up, her bright blue eyes openly curious in a way that did nothing to improve Slade's mood. Without watching Cory Haines cross to the elevator, he shut his door smartly. He'd get Mrs. Minglewood to pull the files on the two properties and to check out Haines Landscaping later on. Right now he needed to put an interview that had been as frustrating as it had been interesting right out of his mind and concentrate on the plans for the waterfront.

But the printouts failed to hold his interest. Restlessly he strode over to the window. The rain had changed back to snow, big wet flakes falling from a sodden sky. It was time he went back to Toronto, he thought moodily. Back to his head office and his apartment and his friends.

Maybe he'd go and see his mother after work. She always cheered him up.

Delicate and elusive, a woman's scent hung in the air, mocking him with all that was missing in his life.

Lavinia Hargreave had remarried after Slade's father had died of a heart attack: an odd death, Slade had often thought, for a man who had given little evidence of having a heart. His memories of his father were of lacks and absences, of coldness and distance, of a quintessentially military man, phobic about emotion and intimacy.

In consequence, Slade had been happy when his mother had married Wendell Hargreave, a retired and rather famous antiquarian bookseller who loved poetry and gardening. Lavinia had blossomed in the eleven years they had been together, and Slade had genuinely mourned Wendell's death, ironically also from a heart attack. Wendell and Lavinia had owned fifty acres on St. Margaret's Bay; only two weeks ago Lavinia had rented it to a university professor and his family and had bought herself a small bungalow in the city. Because she was only gradually getting settled, he'd decided to stay in a hotel this trip.

She opened the door to her son and ushered him in. "You look tired," she said.

He flicked a glance at himself in the ornate antique mirror that overpowered the narrow hallway. Dark brown hair with a tendency to curl, gray eyes, cleft chin—he'd seen it all a thousand times and had never understood why women—secretaries, sophisticates, and sweet young things—all seemed to find him irresistible. "I need a shave," he said.

"You need a holiday," she said tartly. "You work too hard."

They had had this discussion before. "Yes, Mum," he said, kissing her cheek. "You should sell that mirror; it doesn't suit the house."

"The house suits me and the mirror stays. Wendell was very fond of that mirror."

Without asking, she poured him a Scotch and water. Taking a hefty gulp, Slade broached something that had bothered him ever since he'd arrived in Halifax last week. "You could have bought a much bigger house than this, Mum—you didn't even touch that account I set up for you."

Lavinia added a generous dose of Coke to some dark rum; the rum, she always said, was the excuse to drink the Coke. Smoothing down her flyaway white hair, she said, "You know me—I'm much too strong-minded to be dependent. And far too old to change."

"I hope you didn't rush your decision to move."

"I wanted to do it before I was forced to, Slade. Retain an element of choice. There are no stairs in this house, and I'm near a library, a bookstore and a delicatessen. Plus I can take a cab to the theatre and the symphony." She raised her glass in a toast. "I'm really very happy here. Have some chips."

Lavinia didn't believe in cholesterol. He took a handful, smiling at her affectionately, recognizing as always how grateful he was to her for giving him unstintingly the love his father had withheld. "You'll have to do something with the garden."

"Sod it."

"I beg your pardon?"

"Grass, Slade. Grass. No fuss, no muss."

"But you had such a lovely garden in Seaview."

"Change is the essence of life," she said grandly. "Growing old, so someone told me recently, is not for sissies."

"No one would call you a sissy," he said, and suddenly remembered Cory Haines's defiant brown eyes. She wasn't one either. Lavinia, he was almost sure, would like Cory Haines.

Not that they'd ever meet.

"All this nonsense about golden years—I don't see what's so golden about arthritis and all your friends starting to die off. Poppycock." Then she eyed him over the rim of her glass, hesitating uncharacteristically. When she spoke, her voice, for the first time, showed her age. "I probably shouldn't say this . . . but before too long I'd love to be a grandmother again."

"*Don't*, Mum!"

"It's been two years now."

"Yeah . . ." Slade shook his head from side to side, like an animal that had been hit hard and unexpectedly by someone it trusted. "It still seems like yesterday."

"You can't hide in your job for ever."

"I suppose not." He managed a smile. "If I meet someone, you'll be the first person to know."

"You won't meet anyone until you let your guard down; that's as obvious as—as that mirror in the hallway. And now I really will be quiet; I can't stand interfering mothers. Please will you help me move the mahogany bureau in my room?"

The mahogany bureau weighed at least two hundred pounds. "Sure, I'll help you," said Slade, and drained his drink.

An hour later, having moved the bureau, put up curtain rails and unpacked some books, he was on his way, driving carefully down the slick, wet streets. His mother had never mentioned the lack of a grandchild before today. He wished she'd kept quiet about it. Pressure in that department he didn't need.

Feeling unsettled and out of sorts, he decided to drop into the squash club, where he'd purchased a guest pass the day after he'd arrived. It was round robin night; he'd be bound to find a partner.

Before he changed, he checked the schedule by the desk. Tom MacLeod and Bruce Waring were here tonight; he'd played with both of them before. Then another name leaped out at him from the pencilled list. Cory Haines. She'd signed up for a court at seven tomorrow morning with someone called Joe Purchell.

He stood still, his memory calling up her face, so changeable and so vividly alive. Somehow he wasn't surprised that she played squash, a game that demanded lightning-swift reactions, total concentration and a high level of fitness. Besides, she lived not far from here; he'd discovered that when he'd checked out her company before he'd left the office. Not to his surprise, her business was healthily in the black.

Frowning, he headed for the locker rooms.

At seven-thirty the next morning, on his way to the office, Slade pulled into the parking lot at the squash club. He'd slept badly again. His dreams had been blatantly sexual and when he'd woken at about six he'd remembered all too clearly the woman who had cavorted with him on peach-colored satin sheets with such enthusiasm and expertise. Cory Haines. Naked, beautiful and incredibly inventive.

He could control most aspects of his life. But he couldn't control his dreams.

He slammed the car door and took the steps two at a time. Then he strode along the upper gallery that offered a view into the courts below. When he came to the end court he stood back, so that he could see without being seen.

They were rallying, both players covering the hardwood floor with speed and precision, the ball thwacking against the walls like miniature gunshots. Then Cory maneuvered her partner into the back of the court, raced for the front and placed a gentle drop shot into the corner. The man gave a yell of frustration that echoed off the white-painted walls and Cory laughed, a full-bellied chuckle of delight. "My serve," she said, flipping the ball into the air with her racquet.

She was wearing regulation white shorts and T-shirt, her hair in a thick braid down her back. As she stood poised to serve, Slade could see her breasts heaving and the sweat trickling down her neck; her legs were long, their grace in no way lessened by the taut calf muscles. Involuntarily his body hardened in response.

Scowling, he flicked his gaze to her partner. Joe Purchell was taller than Cory, boasted a crop of black curly hair and was extremely good-looking. He was also several years younger than Slade and, by the look of him, in better shape. Slade disliked him on sight.

The rally began. The two players were equally matched, Cory making up in intelligence what she lacked in reach. When the score had been stuck at seven-all for nearly five minutes, Slade left as unobtrusively as he'd arrived.

She played to win. But she also played for the sheer joy of the game. And she was every bit as seductive in the squash court as she'd been in bed in his dreams.

He gunned the car out of the lot and drove to the office, his mouth set in a grim line. The smartest thing he could do was say no to her proposal. A flat no. That way he wouldn't have to see her again. Because the last thing he needed was to be lusting after a woman who almost undoubtedly was involved with someone else. Especially a woman as intense, intelligent and heart-wrenchingly beautiful as Cory Haines.

A woman like that wasn't on the cards for him.

CHAPTER TWO

ONCE in his office, Slade plugged in the coffee machine and spread out the plans for the harborfront, forcing himself to concentrate. Years of discipline came to his rescue; when Mrs. Minglewood tapped on his door to tell him it was ten twenty-five, he'd figured out what was wrong with the boardwalk and had come up with an inventive and ingenious way round the parking problem. Feeling well pleased with himself, he ran downstairs to meet Cory.

The snow had melted and a pale, unconvincing sun was bathing the street in an equally pale warmth. He'd tell her that on reflection he'd decided against her proposal; this would save both of them the time and trouble of inspecting the two sites. Then he'd forget about her. In a couple of weeks he'd be back in Toronto, where he belonged.

Ten-thirty came and went. Ten thirty-five, then ten-forty. Anxiety began to gnaw at his gut; somehow he was sure she wasn't a woman to be late. Then at ten forty-three a small green truck with "Haines Landscaping" emblazoned in gold on its side panels sneaked in between two cars and drew up at the curb with a jolt. Cory leaned over and unlatched the door. As Slade pulled it open she said incoherently, "I'm so *sorry* I'm late; I'm never late; my mother had a thing about punctuality and it's ingrained in me. I can't stand keeping someone waiting... I do apologize, Mr. Redden."

18

He'd intended to stand firm on the sidewalk and deliver his speech and then go back to the office. Instead Slade found himself climbing into the truck beside her, his eyes glued to her face. She looked pale and distraught, a very different creature from the woman he'd watched at the squash club only three hours earlier.

Watched? Spied on would be more accurate. "What's wrong?" he rapped.

"Nothing! I told you, I just hate being late."

"What's wrong, Cory?" he repeated.

It was the first time Slade Redden had used her first name. And it was quite clear he'd sit there until she answered him. Cory said rapidly, "The reason I'm late is because my best friend had a baby this morning—her second. I got the message when I got to work, so I had to rush to the hospital, and then I was late for my other appointment." She gave a weak giggle. "A retired RCMP inspector whose ideas on punctuality would rival my mother's."

"And your friend? Was everything OK?"

"Yes! Yes, of course."

"You don't look particularly happy about it."

Her head jerked round. He saw far too much, this man with the cool gray eyes. Trying to subdue the storm of emotions that had been rampaging through her body ever since she'd seen Sue at the hospital, Cory snapped, "Of course I'm happy for her."

"Yeah? Could have fooled me."

In a loud voice she said, "I'm *very* happy...she has a lovely eight-pound boy. I'm extremely happy." She scowled into her rearview mirror and pulled out into the traffic with scant regard for the clutch. "We'll go to Cornell Street first."

Slade had no idea what was going on, other than that she looked like a volcano about to erupt. He said mildly,

"You know, that's the first time in our acquaintance that you've been less than truthful with me."

"Mr. Redden, I'm—"

"Slade, please."

Cory was unable to think of any diplomatic way to get him off her case. She couldn't possibly explain all her tangled and contradictory feelings to him because she didn't understand them herself. She said in a clipped voice, "My personal life is just that—personal. I would never have told you about Sue if I hadn't been late."

Why did he feel as though she'd slapped him in the face when she was only verbalizing something he fully subscribed to? Business was business, and to mix the personal with it was a bad mistake; he'd learned that very early in his career. So what the hell was he doing sitting in this truck when all his instincts had urged him to cut the connection with her?

Not sure whether he was angrier with her or with himself, Slade said tersely, "What sort of time frame are you looking at for these projects?"

With evident relief she said, "I'd get at them as soon as possible. Spring is a really busy time for me, but I've hired a couple of extra helpers along with my right-hand man, so I'd be able to handle it."

Was Joe Purchell her right-hand man? And what was that if not a personal question? "So the gardens could be available for this summer?"

"Absolutely." She swung down a side street and parked near a corner lot decorated with rubble and a large "For Sale" sign. Her nerves vibrating like piano wire because the next half hour was crucial, Cory slid down from the truck in her neat khaki trousers and work boots and led the way across the street. "I'd make evergreens a priority, so the park would look good in winter," she said eagerly. "But you can see how the maple would provide a lot of shade in summer. I think a couple of winding paths would be a good idea—with lots of benches.''

He glanced around. "Would vandalism be a problem?''

"I've thought of that.'' Enthusiasm warmed her voice. "Rather than beds of brightly colored flowers that might encourage people to rip them up or trample on them, I'd focus on foliage. Hostas and ferns. Low-growing junipers—some of them come in lovely soft blue-greens. Then some middle-height yews and flowering shrubs, plus three or four well-placed granite rocks—a bit of a Japanese influence. I might have a red-leafed Japanese maple as well; they're slow-growing but very effective with evergreens. Here, I've done a computer mock-up.''

He perused the paper she had unfolded, which transformed the deserted lot into a peaceful and harmonious oasis in the city streets. "What about a fountain?''

She grimaced. "That gets pricey. Although it would be wonderful.''

"I have a friend who designs fountains that are both vandal-proof and beautiful,'' he murmured. "The sound of water can be very soothing. I think your focus on foliage is brilliant, by the way.''

Cory flushed with pleasure; he wasn't a man to hand out idle compliments. "The birds would appreciate a fountain, too,'' she said pertly.

"Keep the pigeons and the people happy?''

She laughed. "Right! Have you seen enough? I don't want to make you late for your next appointment.''

On the way to Dow Street, Slade studied her diagram for the gardens. When they arrived, the lot itself was so unprepossessing that he insisted they walk the length and width of it, Cory pointing out the proposed location of the garden plots, the sheds and the playground. He said dubiously, "You'd need tons of topsoil and compost.''

"I have access to both. The sheds would have to be pretty basic. But I'd ask one of the local service clubs to provide the playground equipment; they're very good that way."

The street was as unprepossessing as the lot. The wind, chill from the offshore ice, whirled a discarded candy wrapper into the air as the sun glinted on the splinters of glass that were scattered everywhere. "What about water?"

"Underground hoses. Best way to irrigate."

"But not the cheapest."

His doubts were all too evident. Cory said urgently, "All I'm asking you for is the land, Slade. I read a couple more articles about you last night, about your projects in the poorer sections of Chicago when you were studying architecture. Not all of them worked. But you tried." She tucked a strand of hair behind her ear. "That's all any of us can do."

He stated the obvious. "You care about this. Passionately."

"Yes. Yes, I do."

"I'll deed the land to the city," he heard himself say, "on condition that you let me supply all the topsoil for both sites, and pay for the sheds. I'll also donate some large trees for both places—that can run into money."

"You mean you'll do it?" she squeaked.

With a strange sense of fatality—he didn't often do an about-face the way he had this morning—Slade nodded.

"The park *and* the gardens?"

"Both of them, Cory."

She'd scarcely dared to hope that he'd give the land, let alone add all those extras. Seizing his hands, she danced up and down, her face lit with delight. "That's wonderful! Oh, Slade, thank you; it's so generous of you. I'm so excited!"

The wind blew an empty soda can across the ground; it rattled against the stones. Under Cory's beige shirt with the logo of her company embroidered on the pocket, her breasts bounced up and down. Slade wanted to kiss her so badly that it took an actual effort of will to pull free of her grip and take a step away from her. "I'll look after the legalities with the city," he said formally. "Will you get your lawyer to draw up a contract for the two of us?"

"Aren't *you* excited?"

Yeah, he thought. Sexually excited. Not what you want to hear, Ms. Cory Haines. "Of course I am. I'm just older and better at hiding it."

"Pooh—you're only thirty-four." She stuck out her hand. "Put it there, pardner—we've got ourselves a deal."

Her clasp was firm, her fingers cold. "You should be wearing gloves," he said.

For Pete's sake, he thought, you sound like her father.

"I always forget them. You should see my hands in summer—fancy fashion magazines are not clamoring to photograph them. Every year I buy a pair of gardening gloves, and every year I contrive to lose them the very first day I wear them." She crinkled her nose; excitement was still bubbling along her veins, loosing the guard on her tongue. "It's called regression—I like to make mud pies. The truck, the business cards, the computer designs—they're all just excuses so I can get dirt under my nails."

Amused, feeling her fingers begin to warm in his, he asked, "Weren't you allowed to make mud pies when you were little?"

"*Very* strict parents. Frilly starched dresses and no dirt. My next job will probably be working in a spa slathering people with mud packs."

"Your eyes," Slade said in sudden discovery, "are the color of molasses—that wonderful combination of brown and black. Shiny."

"Well, I must say I've never been compared to molasses before. Gooey and sweet—is that the best you can do?" Suddenly Cory chuckled. "You know what? Your hair is the color of good compost."

"Rotting vegetable matter? Thanks."

"And your eyes," she announced with considerable satisfaction, "are like slate. Gray with gorgeous undertones of blue."

Slade rather liked this game. "Beech leaves in October—that's what your hair reminds me of." His voice deepened. "My stepfather used to grow pink peonies; your cheeks are that color right now."

As if suddenly realizing that they were still holding hands, Cory pulled hers free and babbled, "We'd better go; you'll be late."

"If all the legal stuff's done before I go back to Toronto, I want you to have dinner with me. To celebrate." He hadn't known he was going to say that. Too late now, he thought, with, for the second time, a curious sense of fatality.

"I—I guess that would be all right."

"Good. I'll call you." He glanced at his watch. "Can you get me back to the office in seven minutes?"

They talked about commonplaces all the way back. Cory made no move to touch him again. But before he got out of the truck she gave him a singularly sweet smile and said, "Thank you, Slade. Thank you very much."

"You're welcome," Slade said, and shut the truck door.

It had taken them ten minutes to get back to the office. Nevertheless, he stood on the sidewalk watching her drive away. So much for separating business from the personal. So much for saying no.

He was going to make use of every one of his connections to make sure there were no hitches with the city. Because he very much wanted to have dinner with Cory Haines. No matter what the consequences.

One week later at seven-thirty in the evening Slade was standing in the lobby of what he considered to be the city's best restaurant. Cory hadn't wanted him to pick her up at her house; instead she'd agreed to meet him here.

He was wearing his most expensive dark gray suit and a new silk tie. His hair was brushed into some kind of order and his shoes had a military shine his father would have been proud of. He was nervous.

While he'd had a couple of brief conversations with Cory during the week to sort out the details of their agreement, he hadn't bumped into her at the squash club, nor had she come to the office. This hadn't prevented him from thinking about her almost continuously, however, and dreaming about her with a sexual insistence that, when he woke up, dismayed him.

He wanted to take her to bed, no question of that. Maybe tonight he'd ask her whether she was attached or free. That would be a start.

A start to what? And would she be as beautiful, as full of life as he remembered?

At seven thirty-one the mullioned door of the restaurant swung open and Cory walked through. Slade's heart began to racket around in his chest as though he'd been playing a tournament. He smiled at her, brushing her cold cheek with his lips. She smelled delicious. He said, he hoped casually, "You're on time."

"No more friends with newborn babies," Cory said lightly, and slid her arms out of her coat. What on earth had possessed her to say that about babies? she wondered agitatedly.

They were on her mind, that was why. One particular baby—Sue's—had caused Cory to have a week so full of ups and downs that beneath her surface calm she was as jittery as if she were on her first date. She'd visited Sue three times during the week—Sue was her best friend, after all. But visiting Sue had meant she'd had to hold little Jason in her arms; she'd been deeply upset to learn that pleasure and pain could be so intimately entwined. The last two nights she'd even cried herself to sleep. Her outfit and her makeup were valiant attempts to conceal this fact from Slade Redden's all too discerning gray eyes.

She watched him survey her from head to foot. Her skirt was midnight-blue, slim-fitting and slit up one side; her blouse, of creamy silk, bared her throat and hinted at her cleavage. Her hair, shining with cleanliness, was looped on the back of her head; she only hoped it would stay there. As for her dark blue eyeshadow and matching mascara, she'd operated on the principle that the best defense was offense.

His mouth dry, Slade said, "You look very beautiful."

Infinitesimally Cory relaxed: the mask was working. The maitre d' arrived and led them to a corner table under a collection of old hunting prints, where, as they waited for their cocktails, they talked about the latest developments in their project. Then Slade raised his glass. "To parks and gardens—long may they flourish."

Solemnly they clinked their glasses. With mutual determination they proceeded to discuss the menu, the changes on the city council and the drop in the Canadian dollar. They ate mussels and smoked salmon and drank white wine. Then Slade said, "Dance, Cory?"

The music was lively and because she didn't have to touch him—and was therefore safe—Cory danced her heart out; she had always loved to move to music. The fact that her fiery energy and evident pleasure might be as seductive as actual touching didn't occur to her. Nor could she possibly have known that some of her movements would recall, with uncanny accuracy, portions of her partner's dreams. As the final chord sounded she said exuberantly, "That was fun! Thanks, Slade."

He nodded, his jaw a tight line, and followed her back to the table. But the medallions of pork and julienne vegetables they had ordered were cooked to perfection and slowly the level sank in a bottle of Cabernet Sauvignon. Then the small band started a waltz. "Let's try this one," Slade said.

Normally Cory avoided what she called contact dances. But she'd had rather a lot to drink and more than once Slade had made her laugh until she cried. Confidently she threaded her way through the tables.

At the edge of the parquet floor Slade took her in his arms. Because she was wearing high heels, her chin nearly came to his shoulder; he dropped his head so that his cheek rested against hers. Curving an arm around her waist, he drew her closer, ignoring her slight resistance.

Dream and reality fused. The woman in his arms was the woman who had haunted his sleep for the last eight nights.

But Cory was suddenly and distressingly sober. As she automatically followed Slade's lead, she was attacked by a host of conflicting sensations.

One of the buttons on his jacket was digging into her ribs. He smelled nice. Although she was almost sure he wasn't wearing cologne, a faint scent of lemons overlaid the more earthy scent of clean male skin. She was enclosed in his embrace as a garden was enclosed, safe from the buffeting of wind and storm; yet, simultaneously, she felt as smothered as an evergreen wrapped in plastic, as constricted as a tree trunk girdled too tightly. So tightly that her lifeblood was cut off, she thought, trying to control her uneven breathing.

It was one of her unspoken policies to keep her distance—literally—from men. Because claustrophobia, of the emotional variety, had been Rick's parting—and lasting—legacy to her.

Then the hand that rested on her waist moved lower, splaying itself over her hip and drawing her still closer. Against her groin she felt the involuntary hardening of Slade's body, that indisputable and uncontrollable signal that he wanted her. Panic sliced through her illusive sense of safety; she froze, stumbling over his foot. Raising her head, she muttered, "Slade, I'm not—"

Cursing himself for betraying his need, Slade rested one finger on the softness of her lips and eased away from her. "I didn't do a very good job of hiding that, did I? Sorry. I want you—sure I do. But this is a public place and you're quite safe."

She pulled free, and even in the dim lighting he saw that the emotion tightening her features was fear. Turning away from him, she hurried back to their table, pulled up her chair and buried her face in the dessert menu. Slade sat down across from her. "Come on, Cory. This is the twentieth century, and I'm obviously not the first man you've dated. Take it as a compliment, why don't you?"

"Fine," she said tautly. "I've been complimented. I'm not sure I want dessert; perhaps I'll just have coffee."

Nonplussed, because she was acting more like a Victorian virgin than the capable and confident woman he knew her to be, Slade drained his glass of wine. "So are we going to pretend that nothing happened out there? That I wasn't entirely ready to make love to you?"

The menu slipped from Cory's fingers. Her eyes widened and for a full five seconds she gaped at him as though she had never seen him before. *Make love to you, make love, make love...* The words echoed in her brain as all the pain and longing of the last week coalesced into an idea so simple and so outrageous that she was struck dumb.

"*Now* what's wrong?"

She grabbed her wine glass and tossed back the contents. Then she blurted, "Are you married, Slade? Or engaged? Or living with someone?"

"No, no and no. What about you?"

His answer sank in; his question scarcely registered. It was a crazy idea. Crazy. She should be committed for even thinking it. "This wine is really excellent, isn't it?" she gabbled. "Just a hint of oak and that glorious ruby-red."

Slade leaned forward. "Why did you ask about my marital status?"

"I was just wondering," she said weakly, "that's all."

"Why don't you try telling me the truth? You're a lousy liar."

"My mother used to shut me up in a cupboard if I lied to her—that's probably why. Slade, I had an idea. But it was a totally insane idea and I want to forget about it—please. Let's talk about anything from horticulture to horoscopes, and maybe I will have dessert. I adore key lime pie."

Storing in the back of his mind the image of a small, chestnut-haired girl being confined in the dark, Slade said implacably, "Tell me about your idea. Because it's something to do with me, isn't it?"

"Oh, yes," she said wildly. "Very definitely."

"When you first arrived, I thought you looked tired. That's not considered much of an opener for impressing your dinner date, so I didn't mention it. What's up, Cory?"

So much for mascara. "I don't have to tell you," she said defiantly. "In fact, I'm not going to tell you."

"The restaurant doesn't close until midnight and it's only nine-thirty. I can wait. I could even order another bottle of the wine you so much admired." He gave her a charming smile. "I'd enjoy having to carry you out."

He'd do it, too. She knew he would. And if she kept the idea to herself certainly nothing would come of it.

With the sense that she was embarking on a very flimsy bridge across an extremely deep gorge, Cory said, "All right—you asked for it."

Who knows? she thought. He might even say yes.

CHAPTER THREE

CORY held out her glass to Slade for a refill, shadows dancing over her features from the candle that flickered on their table; she was rather proud to see that her hand was entirely steady.

"I want to have a baby," she said, and heard the words coming from a distance, as though someone else were saying them. "I'd like you to be the father. But I don't want to get married or live with you or even see you again once I'm pregnant."

There was a moment of silence, a silence so charged with tension that Cory frantically wished her request unsaid. Then Slade bit out a single word. "No!" His voice was raw with pain, and she watched as wine sloshed over the edge of her glass.

The stain on the cloth looked like blood. With a superstitious shiver, Cory looked up. The same pain had scored deep lines in his face; his eyes looked like those of a man in hell. She felt as though, rough-handed, she'd ripped a dressing from a wound not yet healed. Yet she'd had no inkling of the presence of the wound, and no idea as to its source or meaning.

Appalled, she whispered, "Slade, I'm *sorry*."

Briefly Slade closed his eyes, knowing he'd revealed something he'd have much preferred to keep hidden. With a superhuman effort he clamped down on himself, forcing breath through the tightness in his chest. Picking up his serviette, he mopped at the spilt wine and said, more or less evenly, "You took me by surprise— that's all."

31

"Come off it! You don't have to tell me what's wrong, but kindly don't pretend that nothing is. I'm not blind and deaf."

Hard-eyed, he said, "Mind your own business, Cory."

She plonked her glass down and said with more vigour than tact, "I bet you're not often taken by surprise, Slade Redden. Especially by a woman."

Pain translated itself to anger. "You take the cake, I'll grant you that. Here's a guy who'll donate a park...might as well get him to make a baby while I'm at it."

"There's no need to be crude."

"I feel crude."

"I told you it was a ridiculous idea!"

"Ridiculous comes nowhere near describing it. And the answer, in case you're wondering, really is no."

The expression on his face when she'd first spoken had given her that message right away. Bright patches of color staining her cheeks, she said, "OK—the answer's no. So let's forget about it. Why don't you order the chocolate pâté? Then I could try it too."

Slade's anger went too deep to be so easily defused. "You drop a bombshell like that and then expect me to discuss desserts?"

"You've given me your answer—there's nothing more to discuss!"

"That's what you think." He'd been ambushed by an old agony, there was no question of that; but now that he'd subdued that particular feeling Slade was aware of other emotions, none of them pleasant. "If you didn't want anything to do with me afterwards, why should it matter to you whether I'm married or engaged?" he demanded. Because that, he thought with ugly accuracy, was where she'd knifed his self-esteem. In the cold-blooded way she was prepared to dismiss him. As if he didn't exist.

Faintly surprised that he should even have to ask, Cory said, "Oh, that wouldn't be moral. To cheat on another woman, I mean."

"Whereas bringing up a fatherless child would be?"

Her temper rising, Cory said, "I don't want to talk about this any more; I thought I'd made that clear."

"We're going to. Whether you want to or not." Viciously he stabbed at the cloth with his fork. "How many other men have you asked?"

"None!"

The odd thing was that he believed her instantly. "So why me? Why don't you ask your squash partner? You must know him a whole lot better than you know me."

"Joe?" Cory frowned. "How do you know about Joe?"

"I have a guest pass at the club where you're a member."

Cory didn't like that, not one little bit. She summoned a smile and looked at Slade through her lashes. "Well, I could scarcely ask Joe. His girlfriend might object."

Slade's jaw dropped. "Oh," he said, and realized he'd been surprised twice in the last five minutes. Maybe Cory Haines was good for him, he thought sardonically. Because she was right—it was a long time since he'd allowed a woman to knock him off balance. "Then why me? You must know a lot of other men."

"They all live in Halifax. I don't want to be tripping over them afterwards. You're from Toronto—although I'd really rather you were from Vancouver. Or Outer Mongolia." Avoiding his eyes, she counted off her fingers one by one. "You're handsome, you're healthy, you're intelligent—good genes, in other words. You don't live here, and—this is important to me—you have principles and you live by them. On top of that, as I discovered on the dance floor, you're not indifferent to me."

"Why, when you've listed all my good points, do I feel as though I've been insulted? I'm not a prize bull, for God's sake!"

She tilted her chin. "This discussion's a complete and total waste of time. You said no—remember?" She gestured to the waiter and when he was standing by their table said crisply, "I'll have the key lime pie and a coffee, please."

"Chocolate pâté and coffee," Slade said. As the waiter turned away, he took a deep breath and said in a more reasonable tone and with entire truth, "I'm curious. You're very young—why this burning need for procreation?"

She said flippantly, "Oh, I probably garden too much. You know, the birds and the bees, all those seeds being planted and coming up in the spring. Fertility, fruition and fecundity."

"Cute, Cory, cute. What's the real reason?"

"I could tell *you* to mind *your* own business."

"You could. You'd even be justified. But I'd really like to know."

Cory stared into her wine, where the candlelight had kindled flames the colour of rubies, until Slade was almost sure she'd forgotten both his presence and his request. Then she whispered, "I'm not so young. I turned thirty-one last October. I've wanted a child for years; I've always known that being a mother would fulfill me in a way my job never could. But I wouldn't be sitting here having this conversation if Sue hadn't had her baby last week.

"Slade, I really was happy for her; of course I was. She's my best friend and a healthy baby is such a miracle." As a sheen of tears glittered in her eyes, Slade fought down the urge to take her hand in his. In the same toneless whisper she went on, "But I envied her too. Envy's a horrible feeling! How can I want something that's hers?''

Considering that only moments ago he'd been furious with Cory, Slade's voice when he spoke sounded oddly gentle. "You're a bright and very lovely young woman...marry someone and have a whole pack of babies." This time he did reach out and cover her hand with his own, feeling tension stiffen her fingers. Her skin was smooth, her bones paradoxically both delicate and strong.

I don't want her to marry someone else, he thought blankly. And explain that if you can, Slade Redden. Because you've got no intention of marrying her yourself.

Earlier, Slade's anger had roused in Cory a matching anger; now his gentleness made her want to cry. She looked down at his lean fingers with their well-kept nails, at the strong bones of his wrist where they emerged from his cuff, and suddenly wrenched her hand free. "I don't want to get married! Slade, I'm sorry I ever brought this up; it was really stupid of me. Can we please change the subject?"

She looked very unhappy. A host of questions hovered on the tip of his tongue. But why ask them? He'd said no, and he'd meant no. No ifs, ands or buts on that one. So she was right. It was past time to change the subject and the one thing he wouldn't do was ask her to dance again. "Here come our desserts," he said. "You can have one spoonful of my chocolate pâté—no more."

With a watery smile she said, "You'll give away real estate but not chocolate, hmm?"

"A man's got to have his limits." After the waiter had gone, Slade put a generous dollop of the rich dark chocolate on his coffee spoon and held it out across the table. With the beginnings of a real smile, Cory leaned forward, closed her eyes, and licked the spoon clean. "Heavenly," she said solemnly.

Her throat was as smooth and creamy as her blouse; her hair was sliding out of its pins, falling in silky strands about her ears. I still want you, Slade thought. Nothing you've said or done has changed that. I want you so badly it hurts.

And what the hell am I supposed to do about that?

Then Cory opened her eyes, smiling right into his. His face was naked with desire, exposed and vulnerable to her in a way that touched something so deeply buried within her that she hadn't realized until now that it still existed. For several seconds, seconds that shivered with intimacy, she held his gaze. Then her lashes dropped and she said with only the slightest of quivers in her voice, "Do you want to try the lime pie?"

"No, thanks," Slade said huskily. "Cory, I don't want to get involved any more than you do."

"Then we won't get involved," she said. "It's simple."

He wasn't sure that anything about Cory Haines—or his reaction to her—was simple. He passed her the cream for her coffee, and with a huge attempt at normality said, "You're thirty-one years old and your company's only been in existence for five years—what did you do before that, Cory?"

She ate a mouthful of pie and rolled her eyes in ecstasy. "Luscious," she said, and in her mind quickly rehearsed an edited version of her working life that would reveal nothing she didn't want it to; her answer would have the added advantage of masking with words that devastating moment of intimacy.

"I took a course in business administration and went to work for a travel agency when I was nineteen." The same year she met Rick. "More or less by chance I started specializing in making the arrangements for women traveling alone, and tapped into a market that eventually led me to manage the agency, and then buy it out.

"I ran it for three years and at first it was enormous fun—I got to go to all kinds of interesting and exciting places. But one day I realized I was spending far too much time in the office staring at a computer screen and dealing with accountants." She grinned. "So I sold it. At a substantial profit, I might add."

"You're not the type to be cooped up in an office."

"Definitely not." She took another mouthful of pie. "That summer I worked as a naturalist in a privately owned resort on the west coast. While I was there, I began to understand that the wilderness is beautiful on its own. Effortlessly. It's the cities that need help. Lots of help. So I took a course in horticultural design and set up my own business here on the east coast." As far from Rick as she could get. "It took a while to get known, but I'm doing fine now."

"So what's next, Cory?"

She laughed and said with the eagerness he'd come to expect, "I'd like to branch out into supplying unusual bulbs and perennials—ones that can survive our maritime climate. A lot of the catalogues are from the west coast and the fruit belt in Ontario—the Atlantic region's been neglected. I'd enjoy doing that."

"I'm sure you'll succeed . . . Do you want some more coffee? Or a liqueur?"

"No, thanks. I should probably head home; I have an eight-thirty appointment tomorrow morning. Let's split the bill, shall we?"

"Why not?" he said agreeably. "Shall we share a cab too?"

"I brought the truck. The passenger seat is full of soil samples I've got to send off to be analyzed—sorry about that."

She wasn't really sorry at all, thought Cory. It was bad enough that she'd asked him to father a child. She wasn't going to crown the evening by inviting him in for a nightcap.

The sooner she got rid of him the better.

They dealt with the bill and the tip, then Cory led the way into the foyer. When she had her coat on, Slade said, "I'll walk you to your vehicle before I call a cab."

Suddenly aware that she was exhausted, Cory also realized there was no point in arguing with him. She walked out into the dark street, pulling her coat closer. "Is it ever going to warm up? I'm only a couple of blocks away."

Slade took her by the elbow. Music drifted from a jazz bar; traffic lights blinked red and green, and a crowd of teenagers jostled them on the sidewalk. Cory walked fast, her heels tapping on the concrete, her one desire to be alone in her little house. She'd made a fool of herself tonight. An utter fool.

When they reached the truck, she turned to face Slade. "I don't expect we'll see each other again," she said. "Thanks so much for all your help with the land, Slade. And good luck with all your other projects."

The wind was playing with her hair; she looked as remote as a statue. He had nothing to lose. Nothing. He cupped her face in his hand, kissed her parted lips and stepped back. "Goodbye, Cory," he said, and to his considerable satisfaction saw that she no longer remotely resembled a statue. Rather, she looked as if she'd like to run him over with her truck. He added blandly, "I'll wait here until you've driven off."

With uncharacteristic clumsiness she unlocked the truck and climbed in. Then she slammed the door, and with a roar of the accelerator drove away down the street.

Slade headed up the hill, his hands in the pockets of his raincoat. He'd eaten too much; it would do him good to walk back to his hotel. Besides, he was too riled up to sleep.

Cory Haines wasn't any more indifferent to him than he was to her.

Not that it mattered. Because he was going to put her right out of his mind.

Two days passed. Slade met with the mayor and the city council, pushed through his plans for the waterfront, inspected several sites on the Bedford Basin, and was approached about a lucrative contract in Montreal. But all his spare moments were spent thinking about Cory. Cory and her idea that he father a child.

Why didn't she want to get married? Was she widowed or divorced? Why had she been so rigid in his arms on the dance floor, so resentful of his kiss by the truck? And why had she chosen him as the sole recipient of her idea?

It was an atrocious idea. So why the devil was he thinking about it night and day?

He knew why. For one thing, if he agreed to it, it would mean he'd be able to make love to her. Assuage the gnawing hunger for her body that had been with him ever since he'd first met her. Maybe then he'd be able to forget her, and she'd stop figuring in his dreams every time he laid his head on the pillow.

The other reason was one he had difficulty bringing himself to acknowledge even in the privacy of his own thoughts. If Cory got pregnant, then a child of his would be alive in the world. His own flesh and blood. Alive. Living and growing and learning.

Cory would be a good mother; he'd stake everything he owned on that. But he, Slade, would be an absentee father, his sole act that of procreation. He wouldn't love the child. He wouldn't even see it.

He'd be uninvolved. Safe.

His thoughts went round and round in his head, like hamsters on a treadmill. But, unlike the hamsters, he couldn't get off the treadmill. Let alone out of the cage.

He spent the weekend with his mother, hanging pictures, carrying boxes up from the basement and painting the smaller of the two bedrooms; on Sunday they drove to Mahone Bay, where she bought herself a lovely antique armoire that he lugged into the newly decorated room and polished with lemon oil.

He planned to go back to Toronto before the end of the week. On Tuesday evening, irritable and out of sorts, he walked to the squash club. He'd booked a court for an hour, which should be long enough to wear himself out; Tom had promised to meet him there. At least when he was playing squash there wasn't time to think about Cory. Nor was he worried about meeting her there; she and Joe always booked for early in the morning.

He played like a man demented, fighting for points he wouldn't ordinarily have contested, risking shots that more often than not paid off, to his surprise and Tom's chagrin. Because he was totally focused on the game, he didn't notice the small crowd of onlookers in the gallery above his head, their heads swiveling to follow the shots. He certainly didn't see Cory among them.

She was standing well back, clutching her racquet to her chest. For a big man Slade moved like greased lightning, his sneakers squeaking on the floor, his racquet digging the ball out of impossible situations; he was constantly on the attack, only rarely allowing himself to be caught defensively. A lot could be learned about someone by watching him play a game. He was, she thought fancifully, playing as though demons sat on his shoulder.

Ten minutes before she was due for her own game, she edged free of the spectators and ran downstairs to the women's locker room.

Slade, had he been asked, might have agreed with Cory about the demons. But Tom, a chemistry professor, had had an extremely frustrating day at work, and at the end of fifty-five minutes Slade won by only a narrow margin. They shook hands, laughing, then Tom wandered over to the benches to talk to one of his students. Slade strode down the narrow corridor towards the locker rooms, swiping at his wet hair with his towel. He had to figure out a way to return those high-lobbed serves of Tom's and keep control of the T at the same time.

He didn't even see the woman until he had collided with her. His elbow brushed the softness of a breast, his arm automatically clutched her round the waist and her racquet dug into his ribs. Then she pushed back from his chest and he saw that it was Cory. She was wearing shorts and a white knit shirt, a sweatband holding back the thick sheaf of her hair. He said blankly, "You only come here in the mornings."

"Joe's out of town. So I'm playing with a woman friend." Slade's T-shirt was soaked with sweat, clinging to his chest so that she could see the curl of dark hair from throat to navel and the jut of his collarbones. He was still breathing hard.

Feeling breathless herself, her palms tingling from the contact with muscles as hard as a board, she heard him say, laughter warming his voice, "You don't want to be within ten feet of me right now. I'm in need of large quantities of soap and water."

This man to be the father of her child? Heaven help her. Cory said ironically, "I was watching you for a while. Remind me never to get in a squash court with you—you'd pulverize me. Do you always play like that?"

"Cory," he said, "after your game why don't you join me at Harold's Pub for a snack and a beer? I've been thinking about your idea."

She said vigorously, "That's one discussion I do not want to reopen."

"I might agree to it," he said.

She paled. "Are you serious?"

"Given certain conditions. I think we should at least talk about it some more."

With a hunted look she said, "I'm late; I've got to go. All right, I'll meet you there in about an hour."

Sweat was stinging his eyes. Slade wiped his face again and headed for the shower. He'd really only opened the way for negotiations, he told himself as he pushed open the locker-room door.

He hadn't made any hard and fast decisions.

CHAPTER FOUR

SLADE had eaten a plateful of nachos with very hot salsa and downed two beers by the time Cory walked in the door of the pub. Several of the men eyed her speculatively, and in a primitive surge of possessiveness Slade stood up, waving to her. She smiled, wending her way through the tables; she looked slim and attractive in jeans and a brown leather bomber jacket. He rested his hands lightly on her shoulders and kissed her, unsurprised to feel tension knot her muscles.

"You're quite a woman," he murmured. "Fifty-five minutes of squash and I still want to throw you down on the floor and make love to you."

Color crept up her cheeks. "The bouncer wouldn't approve."

"Plus the carpet needs cleaning."

With great relief Cory saw the bartender approaching. They ordered burgers and draught beer, then Slade asked, "How did your game go?"

"I lost—couldn't concentrate." She hesitated. "I thought you'd have gone back to Toronto by now."

"Friday afternoon." As their beers were delivered, he paid for them, waited until the bartender was out of hearing, then added, "Although I could delay my flight until Sunday. That way we could spend the weekend together. During which I'd do my best to make you pregnant."

"Slade, I—you've got the wrong idea." As if she knew exactly what she was talking about, rather than having only the haziest of notions from reading popular maga-

43

zines, Cory said in a rush, "There are clinics—it can all be done artificially."

"*What* did you say?"

"You heard."

His eyes narrowed. "I've applied several adjectives to you in our brief acquaintance, but cold-blooded wasn't one of them. Artificially, for Pete's sake!"

"The whole situation's artificial! And I'm not cold-blooded. We hardly know each other, and we certainly aren't in love with each other—how can we make love?"

"Very easily, I assure you. People do it all the time."

"I'm not people. I'm me."

"Then we're both wasting our time. I won't bring a child into the world that way, Cory. You can find someone else."

She couldn't even imagine broaching the subject with someone else. As Slade stared moodily into his glass, she studied his face, seeing as if for the first time the strongly boned jaw, the fan of laughter lines radiating from the corners of his eyes, the cleanly sculpted mouth and cleft chin. Right now he looked older than his years. He's suffered too, she thought humbly, and remembered the pain that had convulsed his features at the restaurant. She said steadily, "I don't want to ask anyone else."

He looked up, his gray eyes unreadable. "But you want me to disappear once you're pregnant."

"That's right. I'd be the sole parent."

"What have you got against marriage, Cory?"

"I'm an independent, financially secure woman. I scare the heck out of eighty percent of men. The other twenty percent have already been snapped up by women quicker on the draw than me."

"I have no doubt there's an element of truth in that. But it's scarcely the reason you react like a gun-shy dog every time I mention the word 'marriage'. Why don't you want to get married?''

Shrugging, she said, ''Been there, done that.''

He said flatly, ''You have this habit of giving flip answers to serious questions. Neat way to keep people at a distance.''

She frowned at him, disliking how easily he seemed to see through her. ''With most men it works.''

''I'm not most men.''

''Ain't that the truth.'' She paused while the waiter put their food in front of them, and reached for the ketchup. ''I was married once. I never want to be married again. And that's all you're getting out of me. Because I'd be willing to bet you're not going to tell me why you've changed your mind. About my idea, I mean.''

''You're right. I'm not.''

''This isn't about building a relationship. It's about making a baby.''

Slade didn't want a relationship; that had been achingly clear to him every day of the last two years. So why did he dislike Cory's honesty so much? He said obliquely, ''I've got a clean bill of health. What about you?''

''Me too.'' She gave a rueful smile. ''It's not even an issue.''

Almost sure she wouldn't answer if he asked why, he said, ''How much financial support will you want?''

Her fork stopped halfway to her mouth. ''None! This has got nothing to do with money.''

He'd sensed that would be her answer. ''Once you find out whether or not you're pregnant, I'll expect you to let me know.''

''I don't want you keeping tabs on me!''

''If you're not pregnant,'' Slade said smoothly, ''you'll presumably want to try again. Won't you?''

And what was she supposed to answer to that? Scarlet-cheeked, Cory said, "I hate talking this way... it sounds so—so utilitarian."

"The same goes for the baby's birth—I'll want to know when it happens."

"I'll think about it," she said shortly.

"I said I had conditions, Cory. There are three more. One, if you ever need help, you're to get in touch with me—I mean that. Two, I'll be contacting you once a year to hear how things are going. And three, once I know you're pregnant I'll change my will so that you and the child will be beneficiaries."

Cory gave up any pretence of eating. "You know what I feel like? A fly that's blundered into a spider's web. At first just one foot's stuck. But the more the fly struggles, the more bits of web it gets entangled in."

"We're not talking about something simple here—a game of squash, for instance," Slade said in a hard voice. "This is a new life you're going to bring into the world—a baby. Not something to be done lightly. If one of the reasons you chose me is because I have principles, you can't expect them to fly out the window when it suits you."

The trouble was, he was right. "Maybe we should give up the whole idea. It's getting more and more complicated." She poked at a dill pickle with her knife and burst out, "Slade, am I wrong to want a baby? I know you're supposed to get married first and then have children. But I hated being married! It seems to have immunized me against falling in love again. I don't want to fall in love. I just want a baby."

Clearly she wasn't talking just for effect; she wanted an answer. But she was asking the wrong man. He was immune to both marriage and children. He said carefully, "Being a single mother won't always be easy."

The pickle was being reduced to a series of neat cubes. "All the other women I know are either settled with families, or else they're having affairs and falling in and out of love. I don't fit; that's part of the trouble."

"Have you thought of adoption?"

"There's a huge waiting list—it could take years. I'm too impatient for that, Slade; I want the baby now. And I know you're right—being a single mother and holding down a job won't always be a bed of roses. But I'm learning to delegate at work. Dillon—my right-hand man—could manage the firm in a year or two, especially if I got into the perennials."

That nasty little jab in his gut—of course it wasn't jealousy. "So why don't you ask Dillon to be the father?"

She gave a rich chuckle. "Oh, no, not Dillon. It's not that he's uninterested in women; he's the very opposite—altogether too interested. A bad case of rampant hormones. When he first came to work for me, I had to set him straight in the first week...and now we're buddies."

Then she sobered, pushing a French fry around her plate. "I have some money put away, from the tourist agency and from when my aunt died. I know Sue would pass on baby clothes and cribs and things." Then she looked straight at him, and said with passionate honesty, "I have so much love to give, Slade. I'd make a good mother; I know I would."

Of all the emotions churning in Slade's chest compassion was uppermost. He said deliberately, "If I didn't believe you'd be a good mother, I wouldn't even be sitting here."

Her eyes filled with tears. As two of them spilled over, trickling down her cheeks, Slade reached over and wiped them away. "You're a good person, Cory. Of course you'd be a good mother."

Two more tears hung on her lashes, then plopped onto her plate. "I don't know why I'm crying," she muttered. She bit her lip. "Yes, I do. It's because you're an honest and decent man, and when you said that to me I—I was touched. Thank you, Slade."

A few brief sentences and he'd been moved to a place he'd neither intended nor wanted. He sat back and took a healthy chunk out of his burger. Swallowing, he said levelly, "I think you should go home and think about each one of my conditions. You might not care for them. In which case the deal's off."

She raised her chin, all her senses reacting to his altered tone. "Are you saying if I do agree to them the deal's on?"

"Yeah ... I guess that's what I'm saying."

Aimlessly Cory put more salt on her fries. "Instead of feeling exhilarated or happy, I feel just plain terrified," she confessed.

Slade wasn't sure what he was feeling. "I'll call you tomorrow evening and you can let me know your decision. Will you be home?"

"Around eight-thirty. I've got an out-of-town appointment after supper." As he nodded, she looked at the remains of her hamburger with repugnance. "I'm not hungry any more. Would you mind if I went home now? I feel as though I've been up for twenty-four hours in a row."

"No problem," he said, pushing back his chair.

As Cory edged her way to the door, Slade realized that in the next couple of days he could well find himself in bed with her. He did know how he felt about that. Just fine.

The following evening Slade took his rented car across town to Cory's house. His excuse was that he didn't want to hear her decision over the telephone. A stronger

motive was his need to see where and how she lived. The
sun had shone all day. His hormones—like Dillon's—
were rampant. He'd gone jogging after work in Point
Pleasant Park and now he was showered, shaved and
dressed in his favorite jeans and a denim shirt, his own
leather jacket keeping out the April chill. Whistling, he
drove along the tree-lined streets.

Cory's house was on a corner lot. It was a small Cape
Cod cottage, painted a soft gray with blue-gray shutters;
a cedar fence edged a garden that, lit only by a streetlamp, was still a visual delight. Snowdrops and yellow
winter aconites spread in drifts beneath an arrangement
of evergreens that his architect's eye could only ap-
plaud. Crocuses, purple and mauve, were coming into
bloom near the south wall.

In the back garden he could discern rose canes, the
shoots of daffodils and narcissi clustering round a pretty
bronzed bird bath, as well as perennial garden shrubs
surrounding the curved edges of the lawn. It would be
very pleasant to sit there on a summer's evening, he
thought.

Not that he ever would.

He walked up the flagstone path and rang the doorbell.

Cory's appointment had been with an energetic young
couple with even more energetic two-year-old twins; the
property had ocean frontage and some wonderful old
oak and pine trees. They wanted a play area, a woodland
garden, raised beds for vegetables and a traditional perennial garden, all of which had geared Cory's imagination into overtime. She'd done some preliminary sketches
and measurements and had promised to get back to them
at the beginning of next week.

Whenever she worked late, she had a leisurely bath
and changed into something comfortable. So when the
doorbell chimed in the downstairs hall she had just put

on her very favorite lounging outfit—a soft knit dress with long sleeves, its gathered bodice hugging her breasts, its full skirt falling to her ankles. Quickly she ran a brush through her hair. It was probably the paper boy; she'd missed him yesterday when she'd been at the pub with Slade.

Half the reason she was wearing this dress, she thought ruefully as she hurried down the stairs, was to give herself courage for Slade's phone call. He wouldn't see it. But she'd know she looked her best.

She pulled the door open. "Oh," she said foolishly. "It's you."

Slade stood still, feeling his heart begin to hammer in his ribcage. Her dress was a swirl of jade-green, her hair a swirl of chestnut. Her feet were bare, and he was willing to bet that beneath the softly clinging fabric she was naked. He said, swallowing hard, "I hope you don't mind—this decision we're going to make seemed too important for the telephone."

"No...no, of course not," she stammered untruthfully. "Come in."

She stood back as he closed the door and stooped to unlace his hiking boots. The hall seemed to shrink. "I was just going to light a fire in the living room," she said. "Can I get you a drink?"

"Black coffee would be fine," he said. "Why don't you let me look after the fire?"

Cory fled to the kitchen. Right now, and despite her profound longing for a child, she would have given everything she owned to replay that dinner with Slade, omitting any mention of anything remotely approaching a baby. She spilt coffee grounds on the counter and nearly dropped the glass carafe on the floor; from the living room she heard the creak as Slade lifted the lid of the log box.

Mad. She must have been mad.

The water gurgled into the pot. She set two mugs on a teak tray, and put out an array of cookies bought from the bakery down the street. Then Slade walked into the kitchen. "Nice room," he said warmly, looking round at the pine shutters and woodwork, the brass accents, and the colorful woven rugs on the terracotta-tiled floor. There was a small pottery bowl of crocuses on the pine table. "I couldn't find the matches, Cory."

"They're under the sink," she muttered. But as she bent to get them he did too. His face was level with hers and all too close; she could see the tiny nick in his chin where he'd cut himself shaving. All the strength seeped from her knees and she was helpless to prevent the heat from creeping up her cheeks.

As though he couldn't help himself, Slade stroked the shining fall of her hair to her shoulders. "I've never seen you with it loose," he said huskily. "You have such beautiful hair—like a banked fire. You should wear it loose all the time."

"It gets in the way when I'm working," she whispered.

This time when he leaned forward to kiss her she was ready for him. His lips were warm against hers, moving with a leisurely confidence that made her tremble deep inside. Maybe, she thought, it wouldn't be so bad. After all, Slade wasn't Rick. She had to keep reminding herself of that.

When he finally broke the contact between them, Cory wasn't sure whether she was glad or sorry. "The matches," she mumbled. "They're on your side of the cupboard."

With sudden intensity he said, "Are we going ahead, Cory?"

"I—please, Slade, let's go into the living room. I can't think when you're so close to me."

"Good," he said, grinning at her so boyishly that she was charmed out of her nervousness.

"Go and light the fire," she said repressively, and levered herself upright.

By the time she'd poured the coffee she could hear the kindling snapping in the fireplace. She went into the living room, noticing that he'd drawn the curtains and lowered the lights. The flames danced on the ceiling. As she sat in the armchair on one side of the hearth, he took the opposite one. She passed him his coffee and the cookies, and said, "I don't understand why you'd want to contact me once a year."

"Just to make sure that everything was going all right. I'm not entirely sure I'd trust you to get in touch if you needed anything—you're very independent."

True enough, thought Cory. "But what if I met someone? Got married? Would you still maintain that contact?"

Slade's stomach contracted as though a giant fist had squeezed it. "I guess we'd have to work that out at the time," he said.

"What I really want is for you to do a disappearing act—go back to Toronto and leave me alone," she said with a violence that sounded exaggerated even to her own ears.

Slade fought down an anger that he would never have admitted had its roots in pain. "Do you think I don't know that? I'm not stupid, Cory. But those are my conditions. Take them or leave them."

She wanted the father of her child to be a man of principle. The price for that was clear: Slade's conditions. One day a year wasn't very often, she thought. She'd have the baby three hundred and sixty-five days a year. Sitting very tall in her chair, she said, "All right. I agree to your conditions."

Slade put down his coffee mug, his expression inscrutable. The flames crackled in the hearth. Then he stood up, put his hands under her elbows and lifted her to her feet. "So we're going ahead," he said. "It'll work out, you'll see."

He was going to kiss her again. And she was committed now; she'd given her word. Cory closed her eyes and with every nerve in her body was aware of the new insistence in his kiss, as though he was claiming her for his own. That was exactly what he was doing—and why not? She'd given him the right to do so. Oh, God, what had she done?

"Relax," he murmured against her mouth, nibbling at her lips. "Why don't we go upstairs?"

"Now?"

"Why not?"

"I—I thought we'd said the weekend."

"I'll put off my flight until Sunday night. So we've got from now until then."

"But..."

He raised his head. "Do you want to get pregnant or not?"

"Yes—yes, of course I do. I guess I'd pictured us at your hotel, that's all."

"This house looks like the center of your life...where better?"

Her house was where she relaxed, her sanctuary from the demands of her job. Slade said sharply, "You don't like me being here, do you?"

Refusing to drop her eyes, she said, "Not really. I've never let anyone in my bed in this house."

He stated the obvious. "You're frightened."

"Frightened" was too mild a word by half. "Of course I am," she said roundly. "You're virtually a stranger to me, Slade."

He said thickly, "Then let's do our best to remedy that. Because making love with someone is one of the surest ways of learning about them."

If he'd intended to reassure her, he'd chosen the wrong words. She didn't want to reveal her secrets to a man as attuned to nuances as Slade.

I've got to do this, Cory thought, clenching her fists at her sides. Or else I'll have to give up the whole idea. Because I'll never have the courage to get this far again. Not with another man.

It's taken all my nerve to get this far with Slade.

CHAPTER FIVE

HER voice higher-pitched than usual, Cory said, "We shouldn't leave the fire."

"I'll close the screen," Slade replied. "It'll be quite safe."

He did so, then reached for her hand to lead her up the stairs. Her knuckles felt like pebbles, her fingers as cold as the sea. "Cory," Slade said forcefully, "we may not be in love, but I—I care about you and I'll do my level best to be good to you. You don't have to be afraid of me."

It would have been just as easy to tell the smoke it didn't have to go up the chimney, Cory thought, and said tonelessly, "My room's at the head of the stairs."

She went ahead of him. Her bedroom had a slanted ceiling set with two skylights through which Slade caught the gleam of stars. The old-fashioned spool bed was spread with a handworked quilt in cheerful primary colors; her bureau was also antique, and a hooked rug lay on the soft beige carpet. A fig tree hung over the bedside table, its leaves casting elliptical shadows on the pale walls. He said appreciatively, "This room looks just like you," sat down on the edge of the bed and started pulling off his socks.

Cory scurried round the other side of the bed and pulled the Venetian blinds shut behind the ruffled sheers. Now what do I do? she thought crazily. I'm not wearing socks. I'm not wearing anything except this dress. And I can't take that off!

Slade threw his socks onto the wicker chair in the far corner, pulled off his shirt and tossed it after the socks. Standing up, he unbuckled his belt and reached for the snap on his jeans. Then something in the quality of the silence in the room alerted him. He looked up. The woman standing on the opposite side of the bed was a woman at bay, he thought. Nervousness he could have understood. But the emotion that held Cory glued to the carpet went far beyond ordinary anxiety.

He padded round the end of the bed, pulled back the covers, then took her hands in his and chafed them. He said gently, "Let's lie down."

She, noticeably, said nothing. As he pulled her down to lie beside him, she didn't actively resist him; but he could feel resistance in every bone of her body. He wrapped his arms around her in a gesture intended to comfort. But his cheek was resting on the smooth fall of her hair, and her soft, full breasts were pressed against his chest. You mustn't rush her, Slade, he told himself. It would be criminal; you can't do that. And he fought down his body's response to her beauty and her closeness.

She was rigid in his arms. Lightly and repetitively he began stroking her back, from the tensely held shoulders down the concavity of her spine to the seductive flare of her hips; and as he did so he dropped little kisses on her hair and her forehead, gentling her as once he had gentled a half-wild stray dog. That dog, he thought wryly, had been the best dog he'd ever had.

Her hands, knotted at his chest, grew warm and slowly uncurled, as petals uncurled to the sun. He let his mouth slide down her cheek, caressing her lips with the same small kisses that gave pleasure, he hoped, without demanding a response. Gradually she relaxed, her breathing deepening, her body curving into his in unconscious seduction. Unable to subdue his hunger for her, Slade eased his hips away, and threaded his fingers through her hair.

"When I was twelve I adopted a stray dog," he murmured. "Its coat was the same color as your hair..." Keeping his voice intentionally low, he started telling her how he had found the dog and some of their exploits, and between his words kissed her again and again, letting his hands roam her waist and the sweet rise of her hip.

She was listening to him, her irises almost black in the chinks of light that seeped through the blinds. As he smoothed her breast under the soft jade-green fabric, her eyes widened in startled pleasure. What he wanted to do was rip the dress from her body. Abandoning his story, bringing all the honed power of his will to prevent himself from doing that, he cupped the softly swelling flesh in his palm and brushed its tip until it hardened beneath his fingers.

"Slade..." Cory whispered, and he saw that her lip was trembling. He kissed her again, this time more deeply, his tongue rippling along her teeth until she opened to him. Slow, Slade, slow, he told himself again, aware that his own shoulders were taut with the effort to hold back.

But then, unmistakably, she kissed him back. It was a shy kiss, one he would have labeled inexperienced had she not told him she'd been married. "Immunized...against falling in love"—wasn't that what she'd said?

Beneath his desire he felt a growing anger towards the unknown husband who had left her so grievously frightened of the act of love; and a surge of protectiveness that she should not suffer in his own arms. So suddenly that he was taken aback, all his struggle for control left him. Replacing it was the simple wish to please her, to bring her happiness and fulfillment. To heal her, he thought fiercely, and slid his lips down the sweetly scented column of her throat.

She was lying very still in his arms. But he was content with that, for it was the stillness of attention and even anticipation, and no longer that of terror. He edged her dress lower on her shoulders, caressing the silky skin with a pleasure totally unfeigned, nuzzling at the hollow of her collarbone. And all the while he was stroking the fullness of her breasts with a hypnotic rhythm that had brought a flush to her cheeks.

For the first time she spoke. Courage overriding the same intense shyness in a way he could only admire, she said softly, "Slade, will you help me take my dress off?"

"I think it'll take two of us," he teased. "We'll have to haul it over your head."

Her smile wavered; but she did smile. "That's not how they do it in the movies," she said.

Halfway it got stuck; giggling, Cory said in a muffled voice, "I must have put weight on... Ouch, don't rip it."

Somehow he got her arms free of the narrow sleeves. Then her tumbled hair and pink cheeks emerged from the long swath of her skirts. He let the dress fall to the floor, and something in the expression on his face as he took in the beauty of her naked body made her say breathlessly, "It's only me, Slade."

He had no answer for her, because he no longer knew what she meant to him. Letting his body speak for him, with exquisitely controlled sensuality he took her waist between his palms, lifting it so that her breasts were drawn taut, drinking in the ivory pallor of her skin, the arch of her ribs and the hollowed navel. Then he kissed her breasts one by one, feeling the triphammer of her heartbeat beneath his lips. Lifting his head, he reached for the zipper on his jeans, dragging his thighs free of the heavy denim.

As he rolled free of her so that his briefs could follow his jeans, he saw panic flare anew in her eyes. "It's all right, Cory," he said hoarsely. "We have all the time in the world and all I want is for you to be happy. I swear I won't hurt you."

He had spoken the simple truth. Her face changed, and with a sudden fierceness that touched him to the heart she reached out and pulled him on top of her, holding him with all her strength. And with all her courage, he thought. She had a lot of courage—more than he could possibly have realized without taking her to bed.

Her slenderness, the grip of her legs wrapped around his, inflamed him. It had been a long time, he thought desperately. Too long. And he had wanted Cory from the first moment he'd seen her.

Grasping at the remnants of his control, Slade kissed her again, a kiss she more than matched. Then, hunger making him clumsy, he nudged her thighs apart with his knee and sought out the crevice in her flesh with his fingertips; she was sleek and wet, more than ready for him, and in passionate gratitude he kissed her parted lips.

Because of the hunger raging through him, a raw and importunate ache that only Cory could quench, he knew that once he entered her he'd be out of control, plummeting to his own climax. His eyes intent on her face, he began stroking her, as though he were adding the most delicate of brushstrokes to a painting almost complete. His reward was in the tiny moans that issued from her throat, the first tentative movements of her hips, the panting of her breath. Then she suddenly cried out his name and, trusting his instincts, he plunged into all the warmth and wetness of her body.

Her nails were digging into his shoulderblades and her face shuddered with a need every bit as tumultuous as his own. Slade drove into her, in and out, fighting for control, and felt deep within her the pulsing of her flesh as she found release. She was sobbing his name, over and over again, clutching him convulsively. And only then did he surrender to his own fierce rhythms, rhythms that spiraled him deeper and deeper until the floodgates burst and he heard himself give a single, raw cry that was both pain and satiation.

He collapsed on top of her, gasping for breath, burying his face in the curve of her throat. Slowly the frantic pounding of his heart quietened. It could have been seconds or minutes later that he became aware that Cory was weeping, in utter silence, tears slipping down her cheeks and dripping onto his face, as cool as raindrops. He said urgently, smoothing her hair back. "Cory, what's wrong? I thought—"

She touched her fingers to his mouth, shaking her head. "I was so afraid," she whispered. "And I didn't need to be. You were everything I could have wished for, Slade—I don't know how to thank you."

It was not the time to ask the reasons for her fear; he said with a quizzical smile, "A pleasure, I assure you."

She settled herself more comfortably in the circle of his arms. She was smiling through her tears as her lashes drooped to her cheeks and her breathing quietened; within moments she was fast asleep, the sleep of utter exhaustion.

Slade half lifted himself on one elbow, studying her features one by one. Beneath brows like dark wings, her lashes clustered under lids that were exquisite ovals of ivory. Her nose was slightly crooked in a way he rather liked; it gave her face part of its character, as did the firm line of her jaw. Her lips, which he'd taken such pleasure in kissing, were soft, sensuous curves. All along he'd thought that all he wanted to do was possess her.

Instead he'd found himself putting her needs before his—and what was that but one of the many faces of love?

Love? He'd loved a woman once, and it had led him to the worst sorrow of his life. He wasn't going to fall in love with Cory.

But their lovemaking, he thought with uncomfortable honesty, had only made him want her all the more.

It was not quite daylight when Cory woke up. For a moment she had no idea where she was. Her cheek was lying on a man's chest, her fingers curled into his body hair; the slow, heavy beat of his heart vibrated in her skull. In sudden terror, as if she had woken to a nightmare that was all too real, she gasped, *"Rick?"* and pushed herself away from him.

Slade said harshly, "Was Rick your husband?"

Her pent-up breath escaped in a tiny swoosh of sound. Slade's dark head was lying on her pillow, not Rick's blond one. Slade, who had brought her such unimaginable delight. "I'm sorry," she muttered. "That's about as tactless as a woman can get, isn't it?" With a small smile she added, "Yes, he was my husband, and I've never slept with anyone except him. So I'm not exactly used to finding a man in my bed first thing in the morning."

"A man who's embarrassingly ready to ravish you," said Slade, and pulled her down on top of him. He could have asked about Rick; it was the logical time. But he found himself reluctant to banish her smile. Reluctant also to inquire more deeply into her life and thereby bind himself more strongly to her?

The tangled hair on his chest rasped Cory's breasts; his mouth was as eager, his hands as skillful as they had been in the darkness last night. But this time she felt only the nibblings of panic, before even they were swallowed up in sensations that made her forget fear and restraint. His lips on her breast streaked her skin with fire; achingly aware of the hardness of his erection against her belly, she kissed him back with unpracticed and unbridled enthusiasm. Then he muttered, "Touch me, Cory—here, and here."

With a hesitancy that spoke volumes, she let her hands explore the breadth of his chest, discovering that other hardness of bone and the smooth play of muscles. Then her hand moved lower, and with a surge of mingled power and pride she heard him gasp with pleasure. As she grew bolder, he matched her touch for touch, kiss for kiss, movement for movement. Her whole body a tumult of desire, Cory arched her hips to take him in, her gaze trained on his face as she leaned over him, her weight resting on her palms.

"Now," she said fiercely. "Slade, now."

Her cry of completion sliced through the dawn light; as for Slade, he knew he'd never experienced such a sense of union, of losing himself in a woman's body. It was as though all the barriers between him and Cory had fallen away, he thought. And yet simultaneously he knew that he couldn't—or wouldn't—put this into words. Holding her close, he shut his eyes.

The light on the other side of the blinds was growing stronger; she'd have to get up soon, thought Cory; she had a nine o'clock appointment. She didn't want to get up. She wanted to stay in bed with Slade for the whole day. While she had traveled an immeasurable distance since last night, she was pretty sure there were a great many detours and side roads yet to be followed, each one of them offering her a freedom she had never contemplated, a bodily joy that was totally new to her.

How could she have changed so much in less than twelve hours? And how much she owed Slade!

She had dreaded the weekend. Now she wasn't sure that the next four days would be nearly long enough.

Maybe Slade could move out of his hotel and stay here in the house. That way they could be together as much as their respective jobs allowed.

As gently as if her fingertip were the petal of a lily, she traced the strong line of his brow, the matching arc of bone beneath his eye. There was a dark stubble of beard on his chin; a very determined chin, she decided, and ran her fingernail lightly over his cleanly carved mouth. Mine, she thought with a tingle of possessiveness. Mine.

Then, as a sliver of ice ran down her spine, she remembered the real reason why Slade was in her bed, a reason that had completely slipped her mind. The baby. Her pregnancy. How could she have forgotten? And why, until now, had it not occurred to her to wonder if he'd succeeded?

She'd been too enraptured by the way he'd treated her, that was why. Too impressed by his sensitivity and restraint: she hadn't been so caught up in all her fears last night as not to appreciate the formidable self-control Slade had exercised over his own needs.

He'd put her needs first. And that had had nothing to do with making a baby.

Not liking the direction her thoughts were taking her, Cory leaned over and turned off the alarm button on her digital radio. Slade stirred, mumbling, "Come here, woman."

She managed a creditable laugh. "I've got to get up. I have an appointment first thing this morning."

He groaned. "I'm expecting a call about a new contract in Montreal, so I shouldn't be late either."

"Who's first in the shower?" she said saucily.

He opened one eye. "Me. Then—providing you have a razor I can use—you can shower while I shave."

"Oh," she said, and even after all the things they had done together in her bed found herself blushing.

Slade began to laugh, great whoops of laughter that made her laugh as well. Then he rolled out of bed and stood up, stretching. His muscles moved as sleekly as an animal's; his big frame was very beautiful to her. He leaned over, kissed her thoroughly and with an enjoyment he made no effort to hide, and strode out of her room towards the bathroom.

That kiss. It had had nothing to do with pregnancy; only as a little girl had she thought you made babies by kissing. Slowly Cory got to her feet. Opening her closet, she gazed at her naked body in the full-length mirror attached to the door.

She was glowing all over, she thought with uncomfortable truth. She even had a pride of bearing that was new. She looked exactly what she was: a woman who had been made love to lengthily and most satisfactorily by a man who had both desired her and cared about her happiness.

None of this had anything to do with a pregnancy either.

Right now, she thought with an honesty as naked as her body, I don't even care if I'm pregnant. Because what Slade has given me is more valuable. He's given me back a part of myself that's been missing for years.

I can't tell him that. It isn't in the bargain.

Her shoulders slumped. Trying to hide a pain that was as invasive as it was illogical, she turned her back on the mirror and made the bed. She then took clean work clothes from her closet, pulled on a housecoat and ran downstairs to plug in the coffee machine. As she came back upstairs Slade called, "Shower's all yours, Cory." Hesitantly she pushed open the door.

Wreathed in steam and nothing else, Slade was standing at the sink. His hair stood up in wet spikes on his head and he looked young and carefree. And happy, Cory thought; relaxed and contented in a way he hadn't looked last night. "Razor?" he queried with the crooked grin that was already so familiar to her.

She pulled open one of the drawers in the vanity and took out her small electric shaver. "It's designed for my legs, not your beard," she said demurely. "Good luck."

He laughed, dropped feather-light kisses on her nose, her cheeks and her lips, then undid the sash on her housecoat and pulled it back so he could look at her. "Slade..." she gasped, trying to stay his hands.

"You're so beautiful," he said huskily, and for a brief moment that made her shudder with pleasure she felt his wet hair on her skin and his lips at her breast. Then he looked up. "What time are you through work today?"

She thought for a moment. "Six or thereabouts."

"I'll take you out for dinner," he said promptly. After the briefest of pauses he added, "Cory, how would you feel if I stayed here rather than at my hotel?"

The uncertainty in his gray eyes touched her in a way she didn't want to analyze. "I'd like that," she said.

"You'd already thought of it?"

"Yes. But I wouldn't have had the nerve to ask you."

The smile faded from his face. "Cory, you never have to doubt your courage. I don't know what's behind your fear, only that it's connected with Rick. I do know you were very brave last night."

"I'm going to start crying again," she muttered.

With a wordless exclamation Slade pulled her to his chest and kissed her hard. She could feel the whole length of his body against hers, and with sudden, primitive excitement knew they would make love again that very evening. "We could meet here before dinner," she whispered.

"An aperitif?"

"I adore them."

"Done." Then he patted her on the bottom and pushed her towards the shower. "Off you go. Or guess where we'll end up?"

"Taking cold showers?" she offered gently.

"You know damn well that's not what I had in mind."

With unexpected intensity Cory said, "I love it when you laugh. Am I wrong to think there hasn't been enough laughter in your life recently?"

"Not wrong at all. Shower, Cory."

Something in his face discouraged further questions. She bundled the soft mass of her hair into a plastic cap and stepped under the stinging hot water. She sang lustily as she lathered herself with soap. When she stepped out, her skin gleaming pink, Slade was shaved, dressed in jeans, and attempting to comb his thick hair into some kind of order.

She stripped off her shower cap and grabbed a towel. This is all so domesticated, she thought blankly. It's as though we're married.

It's not what I expected at all.

"What's wrong?" Slade said sharply.

"Nothing! I—I just can't believe that two weeks ago I hadn't even met you."

"Read Einstein on the relativity of time," he said drily; and, because she was looking frightened again, he walked over to her, lifted the silky weight of her hair in his hands and kissed her as if no one else in the world existed but her.

Eventually he released her. Cory blurted, "What's that kiss got to do with making me pregnant?"

Slade stepped back; he felt as if she'd slapped him hard across the face. For a moment he, who at the office rather prided himself on his fast thinking, could think of absolutely nothing to say.

With passionate regret, knowing she would have done anything to take the words back, Cory cried, "I'm sorry—I shouldn't have said that!"

"We're going to be late, Cory; we'd better get out of here."

His features were as flint-hard as his eyes; he'd retreated to a place she couldn't follow. "There's coffee in the kitchen," she mumbled. "Slade, I'm sorry."

"I'll meet you downstairs."

No more kisses. That was what he meant.

She dressed hurriedly, afraid he might leave without saying goodbye. When she went into the kitchen he was rinsing out his mug in the sink. "Great coffee," he said with an impersonal smile. "I'll make a reservation for seven and pick you up here at quarter to; how's that?"

So there was to be no lovemaking before dinner. She said coldly, "I dislike unilateral decisions when they affect two people."

He said with a softness that carried true menace, "But you've already made a much more important unilateral decision, Cory—you want me to vanish from your life after this weekend. Or had you forgotten that?" Then, jingling his car keys in his hand, he walked past her and took his jacket out of the hall closet. Thrusting his arms into it, he unlatched the front door.

As he swung it open, Cory said inelegantly, "I'm so angry with you I could spit."

He turned around, raising his brows. "I don't think your parents, if they were as strict as you say they were, would approve of that as a way of saying goodbye to your lover."

"They've been dead for years—and they would have been so appalled I had a lover that the spitting would be an irrelevance."

"Your eyes look like firecrackers," Slade said in genuine amusement.

"And at the same time," she added deliberately, "I'm so incredibly grateful to you for last night. Thank you so much."

In her trim beige pants and shirt, her hair braided, she looked very different from the woman who had writhed beneath him in the bed upstairs. He'd hated her comment about pregnancy, and for a very simple reason. She'd been dead right. He wasn't sure anything he'd done in the last twelve hours had been about making Cory pregnant; it had gone much deeper than that.

Not part of the game plan.

"I'll see you tonight," he said, and pulled the door shut.

Cory turned away. For a moment she paused at the living-room door, noticing that the ashes in the fireplace were cold and gray. The fire was indisputably out.

What kind of fire had she and Slade kindled in her bed? And how, after the weekend, would she put it out?

CHAPTER SIX

SLADE had to go back to his hotel and change, so he was late arriving at the office. Mrs. Minglewood eyed his tousled hair circumspectly and said, "An urgent fax from Montreal, Mr. Redden. I left it on your desk."

Slade read the fax, made two phone calls, then called Mrs. Minglewood into his office. "Danvers in Montreal wants me there this afternoon at the latest. Fax and e-mail won't cut it—I'll have to go. Could you make my plane reservations, please? You can cancel my hotel here. And I'll need a limo to the airport."

Claude Danvers was the president of the international conglomerate with which Slade wanted to do business. Duly impressed, Mrs. Minglewood said, "Certainly, sir," and bustled out of the room.

Quickly Slade flipped through the phone book until he found the number for Haines Landscaping. A man answered the telephone. Dillon, thought Slade. The right-hand man with the rampant hormones. Would Cory fall for him now that Slade had taken away her fear of making love? He said crisply, "Please could I speak to Cory?"

"She's out on a call, should be back by eleven or so," the man drawled. "I can give you her pager number if you like?"

He couldn't call Cory in the middle of an appointment to tell her he was leaving the city and wouldn't be back. Danvers had a reputation for ferocious work habits, so the weekend was undoubtedly shot. Next week he had to be in Vancouver. "Have her call Slade Redden

69

as soon as she gets in, would you?" Slade said and reeled
off his office number.

"Sure thing," Dillon said.

Mrs. Minglewood tapped on Slade's door with a choice
of flights. He chose the earlier one, and for the next two
hours they organized the workload he was leaving behind
in Halifax. Then the phone rang on his desk. The number
on the digital display was Cory's. He said politely,
"Would you excuse me, Mrs. Minglewood?" picked up
the receiver and said hello.

"Slade? Cory here."

Her warm contralto voice conjured up her presence
so strongly that for a moment he was struck dumb.
"Slade?" she repeated uncertainly.

"Yeah...I'm here. Cory, I'm really sorry, but I've
got to leave this afternoon." Briefly he explained his
predicament. "The trouble is I'm in Vancouver all next
week, with the strong possibility of a jaunt to Hong Kong
after that."

"Oh," she said. "I see."

"I've worked my butt off for this Montreal contract,
otherwise I'd tell him to get lost."

"I don't think you should do that."

"You sound so goddamned polite! Aren't you
disappointed?"

"Of course I am," she said. But there was no real
feeling in her voice.

"You must know how much I wanted to spend the
weekend with you."

She made an indeterminate sound that could have been
agreement or disagreement. Thoroughly frustrated, Slade
exploded, "There are times I hate the bloody telephone!
But I don't even have time for lunch with you, Cory;
the limo's going to be here in half an hour."

"I have a midday appointment anyway," she said.

Banging his bunched fist on the desk, he said, "I'll fax Danvers and tell him the soonest I can get there is tomorrow."

"No! No, you mustn't do that."

For the first time there was emotion in her voice, and it was unquestionably fear. "You don't care, do you?" he said in an ugly voice. "After all, the odds are good that you've got what you wanted. I'm dispensable now."

"Slade, it's not—"

Too angry to listen, he snarled, "I can take a hint. I'll call you in a month's time to see if you're pregnant. We'd both better hope you are—I wouldn't want to subject you to my presence any longer than necessary."

"You're behaving very childishly," she blazed.

"That's not what you said last night." A discreet knock came on his door. He said, "I've got to go. I'll talk to you next month," and slammed the phone in its cradle with unnecessary force. Mrs. Minglewood came in bearing another fax from Claude Danvers, confirming a three-thirty meeting that afternoon.

The die was cast, thought Slade. Just as well he was getting out of here. Cory Haines spelled danger. Her body intoxicated him, and her emotions were a convoluted mystery he would do best to avoid.

Indirectly, Claude Danvers was doing him a favor.

Cory put down the phone. She should have explained to Slade that Dillon was within earshot during the whole conversation, she thought sickly. But she had been so shocked to hear that Slade was leaving, that she wouldn't see him again, that her brain had shut down.

Montreal, Vancouver, Hong Kong. Meetings with presidents of international conglomerates. He was out of her league.

Anyway, she'd wanted him out of her life, hadn't she? So why was she so upset that he was leaving?

Banging some flower pots together with unnecessary noise, Dillon walked through from the storage area next door into her tiny office. "Do you want these—? You OK, Cory?"

Dillon McDade had eyes the blue of a summer sky, wavy blond hair and a tanned face with very white teeth—a combination that women liked more than was perhaps good for him. He was also kind as long as a good deed didn't seriously inconvenience him, and an exceptionally hard worker. For this last factor alone Cory considered herself lucky to have him. She said, pushing a wisp of hair behind her ear, "I'm fine. A—a friend of mine had a change of plans, that's all."

"A guy, huh?"

"Well, yes."

"Always lots of other fish in the sea," Dillon said sagely.

He was right. Although since Rick's departure she'd never cared for fishing. "I have to be in Tantallon by twelve-thirty," she said. "Are you going to Dow Street?"

He nodded. "The bulldozer's arriving any time now."

"Great," she said. "I'll see you there once I get back."

Dillon ambled off and Cory closed her office door. She had half an hour before she had to leave. Half an hour to rid herself of the dull ache lodged in her stomach and to dump the misery that was sitting on her shoulders like heaped boulders. There was no reason she should feel this way. No reason at all.

Four weeks passed, during which Slade's flip comment to Cory about the relativity of time proved all too true. He was awarded the Danvers contract, and normally would have been excited by the challenge it presented and gratified by its potential to put his company in the top ranks. It rained unceasingly in Vancouver, and the trip to Hong Kong passed by in a blur of skyscrapers, meetings and jet lag. Toronto, when he got home, was basking in an early heat wave.

For the whole four weeks Slade worked harder than he'd ever worked in his life, and whenever he had free time in the evenings he went to the movies. Good and bad, violent and romantic, Hollywood and foreign, he saw them all, sometimes with friends, more often alone, and always with the aim of turning off the ceaseless circling of his brain. The other thing he did was play squash and jog the city streets in an effort to tire his body out so that he'd sleep.

Despite all this activity, time crept by with the slowness of the proverbial turtle, Cory was never far from the front of his mind, and he was sleeping lousily.

For two years he'd done without a woman. Then Cory with her chestnut hair and her crazy idea had penetrated all the barriers he'd so painstakingly built. The barriers had fallen and in the time since he'd left Halifax he'd learned to his cost that he couldn't rebuild them.

He must have been out of his mind to make love to a woman he scarcely knew.

Yeah, he thought. Out of his mind with lust.

His apartment at night was the worst. Alone in his wide bed, he had no defenses against the memories of Cory or against the exigencies of his body. He'd been a fool to think that going to bed with her would cure him of wanting her. Thirty-four years old and that was the best he could do? Where had he been all his life? How could he have been so abysmally stupid?

But even worse than physical frustration and his memories of Cory were his own thoughts. Three in the morning was the time he was most vulnerable to them: his powers of reason and logic did not function at their best in the middle of the night.

It was entirely possible, he knew, that in those tempestuous hours he'd spent in Cory's bed he'd fathered a child. How could he have been so irresponsible? So idiotic? So immoral? Breaking into a cold sweat, he would lie in bed staring up at the ceiling, aghast at what he had—or had not—done. For equally, of course, Cory might not be pregnant.

If she wasn't, he thought grimly, there'd be no repeat of what had gone on in her bed. That decision had already been made. He'd been an utter fool once. He wasn't going to repeat the same mistake. But oh, God, how he wanted her.

His imagination could run rampant with only the slightest encouragement, presenting him with graphic pictures of their lovemaking that were a torment to him. Abstinence, he was discovering, no longer suited him. But no one other than Cory would do. He was so sure of that that he didn't even bother dating anyone for his many trips to the movies.

One of the worst things about all this was that he couldn't tell anyone. Not his friends, and certainly not his mother. The first time he spoke to her on the phone when he got back to Toronto, he felt as though every word he said was laden with deception. His mother, so she'd said, would love to have another grandchild.

Four weeks to the day after Slade's precipitate departure from Halifax should have been a day better than most: Danvers had complimented him on his work and the first phase of a downtown renewal project in St. John was completed right on schedule. A month, thought Slade. He'd told Cory he'd phone her in a month. Two more days. That was all.

Had he or hadn't he fathered a child? Was she or wasn't she pregnant? Feeling like some kind of modern-day Hamlet, he walked back to his apartment at nine that evening after watching an incredibly boring movie that had been billed as the season's best comedy and during which he hadn't laughed once.

It took Cory to make him laugh. Really laugh.

As he took the stairs to his apartment two at a time, he recognized something else that had been staring him in the face for the last twenty-eight days. The one thing he no longer felt was the kind of dull indifference, the aching void that had underlain so much of his life for the past two years.

He felt irritatingly and painfully alive. And he didn't like it one bit.

The cleaners had been in his apartment that day; it looked immaculately tidy and as sterile as a movie set. As though a magnet were dragging him, he walked over to the telephone. He wasn't going to wait any longer. He couldn't stand one more night of suspense.

The truth. He had to know the truth.

He didn't have to look up Cory's home number; it was engraved on his brain cells. He dialed quickly and with a hammering heart heard the first ring. The phone was in Cory's kitchen, that pleasant room that even at night had hinted of sunshine. There'd also been a phone by her bed; he remembered that, too.

Two rings. Three. Then, with a metallic click, the answering machine cut in. Cory's voice, sounding strangely diminished, said, "We're unable to take your call right now. Please leave a message after the beep and we'll get back to you as soon as we can."

The plural pronoun, he knew, was a sensible precaution for a woman who lived alone. "But what if I met someone?" she'd said to him that last evening, and his gut had screamed a protest. With a peremptoriness that sliced through his thoughts and jangled his nerves, the beep sounded. Into the silence he said, "Cory, will you please call Slade?" and bit off the eleven digits. "Anytime before midnight, Toronto time."

He banged the receiver back on the hook and ran his fingers through his hair. It was ten o'clock in Halifax. Where was she? Who was she with?

He had to stay here now waiting for her to call; he'd never been good at waiting; he'd inherited his father's impatience. He flipped through the channels on the TV and watched the last half hour of an old war movie. The sitcom that followed was more asinine than the movie he'd seen earlier. After changing into shorts and a T-shirt, he went into the den where he had a weight machine and a treadmill for those times in the winter when he couldn't jog outdoors. His body, he thought wryly, had never looked so good.

Where the devil was she? Why hadn't she phoned?

Cory had gone to see her friend Sue that evening. Spring had finally arrived in Halifax; scilla and species tulips poked their heads among the primroses in the rock garden that Cory had designed for Sue and her husband Ralph. As dusk blackened the branches of the trees, a robin warbled from behind the house.

Ralph was out of town on business and the two children were settled for the night; Cory had made sure of that before she arrived. Taking a deep breath, she rang the doorbell.

Sue opened the door and hugged her. "Lovely to see you. After a day with my two little monsters, I'm in dire need of some adult conversation. How are you?"

Adult conversation was exactly what Sue was going to get, Cory thought ruefully, and said with true affection. "You look wonderful, Sue; motherhood agrees with you."

"For that," Sue said, "you get an extra piece of chocolate cake. Can you believe I actually had time today to make a cake? Want tea?"

Sue's hair was a mass of short black curls, and although her blue eyes were shadowed with tiredness she looked what she was: a happy woman who knew herself to be happy. "Love some," Cory said.

Sue and Ralph flirted with modernism; their kitchen was a stark black and white, and Cory was glad when Sue took the tea and cake into the family room. Toys and a playpen, books, Ralph's old model airplanes and Sue's wood carvings made a cheerful clutter with which Cory felt much more at home. Sue poured the tea and rattled off the events of her day. Then she laughed. "Sorry, Ralph's been gone since yesterday, so you're getting the full brunt. Your turn."

Cory had planned a circuitous approach, perhaps as much for herself as for Sue; she still wasn't sure she really believed what she'd been told. She said, "I'm pregnant."

"What?"

"I went to the doctor today and he confirmed the result of a kit I'd bought. I'm due at the end of December."

Sue's face was a study in conflicting emotions. She said faintly, "Are you happy about this?"

With a tiny smile Cory said, "Ecstatically."

Impulsively Sue got up and gave Cory another hug. "Then I'm happy for you. But Cory—who's the father? I didn't know you'd been seeing someone."

This was the difficult part. And why should she feel that, subtly, she was betraying Slade? It made no sense. "You know me better than anyone," Cory said in a rush. "You know I don't want to get married again. But for as long as I can remember I've wanted to be a mother. It wasn't on the cards with Rick, and just as well. But last month I—I met a man who doesn't live here, and he agreed to—to make love to me and then let me be a single mother if I got pregnant. And that's what's happened. I am."

"He's going to support you, though," Sue said confidently, sitting down in her chair again. "Financially, I mean."

"No. I don't want him to."

"Cory!" Sue exclaimed. "You mean you'll never see him again?"

"That's right."

"Did you like him?"

"Yes." Cory bit her lip. "He's a good person—that's one reason I chose him. But I don't want to marry him."

"Did he ask you?"

"No! It was the equivalent of a one-night stand." And why did that sound so tawdry when in fact it had been one of the most beautiful experiences of her life?

Sue was scowling. "He's married. Or otherwise attached." Cory shook her head. "Does he know you're pregnant?"

"Not yet. I only found out myself this afternoon. Sue, I don't want to talk about him! I'm going to have a baby; that's what's important."

Sue put down her cup. "We've never talked about this before and it's really none of my business—but I've always had the feeling you weren't overly interested in sex, Cory. Because of Rick, I suppose." She paused then said delicately, "How was it, going to bed with this man?"

Ridiculously Cory felt like crying. "It was wonderful," she quavered. "But so what?"

"I think you should give serious thought to building a relationship with him. Being a mother's hard work, and lots of days I'd be climbing the wall if I didn't have Ralph to turn to. He's a marvellous father—I knew he would be, and that's one of the reasons I married him." Sue grinned. "That, and his legs. I do have to admit that Ralph's ankles make me weak."

"But I—"

Sue overrode her. "I could bring up Amy and Jason myself if I had to. Of course I could. But it would be difficult and awfully lonely. And Amy adores her father—when he comes home from work is one of the high points of her day."

Cory said hotly, "Are you saying single mothers are no good just because they're single?"

"No," Sue said forcefully, "that's not what I'm saying. But if you have a choice here, Cory, and this man is a good man, you ought to look very hard at what you're doing."

"I never want to get married again! I hated it."

"Not everyone's like Rick. Ralph isn't."

"Well, of course he's not."

"Rick was the problem. Not marriage."

With frantic truth Cory said, "It was feeling he had a claim on me, having him around all the time, feeling trapped and penned in. And frightened, too, if I'm to be honest, because when I wanted him to leave he wouldn't. All those things. I'm scared to death of letting a man get that close to me again."

"You've never even talked to me about Rick before tonight."

Cory said raggedly, "I'm only telling you now to explain why I don't want to get married."

In true distress Sue said, "I don't mean to badger you. You're my dearest friend and I only want what's best for you."

"This baby is what's best for me. Truly, Sue."

Sue's face relaxed into a smile. "In that case I'll get off my soapbox. Tell me how you're feeling."

"Scared. Excited. Astounded. Amazed."

"That'll do for a start." Sue chuckled. "I can lend you lots of books. And by December Jason won't need the bassinet any more, and he'll have outgrown a lot of his baby clothes. In fact, there are a few things he's outgrown already; let's go and find them. Oh, Cory, we'll have such fun together.''

Five minutes later Cory was standing by the nursery door holding three little vests and two sleepers, all of which looked incredibly tiny. Tears running down her cheeks, she said, "It's nuts to cry when I'm so happy."

"Hormones," Sue said. "I go up and down like a yoyo in the first three months."

They ransacked Sue's bookshelves, then, when Jason woke for his feeding, Cory changed him. Once he'd settled, they had another cup of tea. At ten past eleven Cory said, "Goodness, I must go; you need your sleep. Thanks so much for everything."

"You're welcome. And call any time."

Cory drove home and unlocked the front door, carrying her little bundle of baby clothes as if they were rare Himalayan poppies. As she put them down on the kitchen table she noticed her answering machine was blinking. Dropping her jacket over the back of a chair she pressed the "play" button.

Deep and resonant, Slade's voice surged into the room. Cory sat down hard in the nearest chair, feeling as though a tidal wave had just slammed into her.

He couldn't possibly have known that today was the very day she'd found out she was pregnant. Could he?

With a superstitious shiver she gripped the edge of the table, needing the smooth, unyielding wood under her fingertips to give her a sense of reality. Reality was the familiar kitchen, the visit with Sue, the unalterable and miraculous change in her body. Not Slade. Not the trembling in her knees, not the ache of desire that had swept over her, as imperious and unstoppable as a wave of the sea.

It wasn't the first time in the last four weeks that this had happened. Cory had spent only one brief night in a man's arms, yet that had been enough to bring her body to life in a way she could neither control nor subdue; for the first time since she'd hired him, she'd had the glimmerings of sympathy for Dillon. Except that Dillon seemed entirely happy pursuing a whole variety of women, while she couldn't imagine making love with anyone but Slade.

She'd phone Slade right now and tell him she was pregnant. Then, until the baby was born, she wouldn't need to have any further contact with him. Quickly, before she could change her mind, Cory replayed the message, copied his number down and dialed.

On the third ring he picked up the receiver. "Slade Redden," he barked.

She swallowed. "It's Cory. I got your message."

For a couple of seconds that felt like for ever the silence was broken only by his harsh breathing. Then he said, "Sorry, I've been lifting weights; that's why I'm out of breath."

It's nothing to do with me, in other words, thought Cory, and said politely, "How are you?"

"The last four weeks have felt like ten years," he said trenchantly. "Are you pregnant?"

"Yes," she said.

There was another charged silence. "Were you planning to let me know?"

"I only found out today!"

"I see. When are you due?"

"After Christmas."

"How are you feeling?"

As though I'm drowning, she thought with desperate truth. "Fine," she said.

"That answer's about as revealing as a blank page in a book!"

"How are you feeling, Slade?" she retorted.

"As though I'm being torn apart. I should never have agreed to go to bed with you; I was a damned fool."

And this was the man Sue thought she should marry? "Well, it's too late now," Cory said, and even to her own ears sounded heartless. She added hastily, "I promise I'll let you know when the baby's born."

"And that's that?" he said with dangerous softness.

"That's the agreement we made."

"I don't think you have an emotion in your body," he grated.

"Slade, I'm not going to fight with you on the telephone! If you haven't got anything more positive to say, let's end this."

"End it?" he said softly. "But Cory, it's only just beginning."

There was a click in her ear, and then the hum of a disconnected line. "Oh!" Cory said out loud to the empty room, and banged the phone down. "You're the most aggravating, arrogant man I've ever met and I don't care if I *never* talk to you again."

Grabbing the box of tissues from the counter, because for the second time that day she was crying, she stalked upstairs to bed.

And the next day, because he was the person who saw her the most, she told Dillon she was pregnant.

"No kidding?" said Dillon, his jaw dropping. "Didn't know you had a boyfriend, Cory."

"I don't. I'm going to be a single mother. I'm telling you about it because I won't be lifting the largest bags of topsoil and compost any more."

"No way," said Dillon, regarding her as warily as if she might give birth at any minute. "That morning you looked so awful; was that the guy?"

One of the things that made Dillon such a valuable employee was his prodigious memory for detail. "I don't want anyone knowing the father's identity," Cory said carefully.

"Not right that he should leave you holding the bag."

"It's fine with me, Dillon."

He didn't look convinced. "You planning to keep the business going?"

"Definitely. The baby's due in December, so by the time we get busy in the spring I'll be back on my feet."

"Well, you look after yourself," he said dubiously. "By the way, the carpenters are showing up at Dow Street this afternoon."

The carpenters that Slade was paying for. "Good," Cory said, and wished that just for once someone would greet the news of her pregnancy with unadulterated delight.

However, as the days passed and spring merged into early summer, Sue and Ralph were more than supportive, while Dillon refused to allow her to carry so much as a flower pot, treating her like an extremely fragile seedling. She didn't hear from Slade again, despite the implicit threat in his last comment, and told herself that she was glad. But she dreamed about him much too frequently for her peace of mind, and often woke in the darkness reaching for him, her body filled with a raging hunger for his embrace.

In her ignorance she'd thought being pregnant would put an end to physical desire. That this wasn't so was one of the many lessons of those first few weeks. The next in order of difficulty, she soon decided, was morning sickness, which, belying its name, usually attacked her in the afternoon; she moved her computer into her house, scheduling her appointments for the mornings and working at home on designs and orders in the afternoons.

So it was eleven-thirty one morning in early June when Cory arrived at the home of a Mrs. Lavinia Hargreave. The bungalow was small but charming, the garden an uninspiring expanse of lawn. The woman who opened the door to her had piercing gray eyes in a face full of character, which was crowned by a head of flyaway white hair; Cory liked her immediately and couldn't equate either the face or the hair with the tidily mown grass.

"Why don't we go right into the garden?" Mrs. Hargreave said. "If you can call it that." She put her head to one side. "It reminds me of a cemetery waiting for its first customer. And since I have no intention of popping off yet I've decided to do something about it. My dear husband Wendell was an avid gardener, and I missed him so much when I first moved here that I didn't have the heart to plant so much as a pansy. But I think he'd like me to have a garden. Just as long as you'll do the work, dear?"

"I can design and plant the garden, and for a monthly fee we do upkeep as well," Cory said.

"Wonderful! Tomorrow's my birthday, so the timing's perfect...what better present could I give myself?"

"Sounds good to me." Cory smiled. "Tell me about your other garden."

As the old lady talked, Cory gained a picture of the happiest of marriages and of a garden that was a combination of formality and the fortuitous accidents that could make the difference between a merely pretty garden and a beautiful one. She got a long piece of orange rope from her car—Dillon had the truck that morning—and laid it on the grass, outlining various possibilities for beds; she stuck stakes in the grass for small trees and shrubs.

Suddenly Mrs. Hargreave cocked her head. "I believe I just heard the doorbell; I'll be right back. It might be the postman; I'm expecting a birthday parcel from Toronto."

Cory stayed where she was, running her tape the length of the fence and jotting down the measurements in her notebook. Quickly she sketched in the location of the neighboring trees and assessed the level of shade. Then she heard voices coming towards the back door, a man's deep voice mingling with Mrs. Hargreave's softer tones.

"Lovely to see you, dear. What a nice surprise, and just in time for my birthday. My present to myself, by the way, is to do something with the garden."

"Got bored with grass, did you? I'm glad to hear it."

She knew that voice, Cory thought, terror-stricken. It was Slade's voice. But it couldn't be. Slade was in Toronto.

Not in Halifax visiting one of her customers.

CHAPTER SEVEN

CORY stood rooted to the ground under the branches of a newly leafed silver birch, her heart racing like a frightened bird's, her face dappled with shade; she was wearing the beige short-sleeved shirt and dark green walking shorts that were her working uniform for summer. In the split second before Mrs. Hargreave came out of the door, she made a frantic effort to compose her face to something approaching ordinary politeness.

"Just this morning," the old lady was saying, "I've had someone come here to give me advice... This is Cory Haines, Slade; she's a landscape designer. Cory, I'd like you to meet my son, Slade Redden."

"My son, Slade Redden"... Feeling as though the very first grave had indeed opened at her feet and she had fallen into it, Cory croaked, "How do you do, Mr. Redden?"

He was standing behind his mother, white with rage— a rage so intense that she took an instinctive step backward. But then by a superhuman effort he forced it down, and only she saw the muscles stand out in his throat and the clench of his fists at his sides. He said, the timbre of his voice almost normal, "My pleasure."

Mrs. Hargreave said brightly, "You won't know the garden the next time you come, Slade—you wouldn't believe what good ideas Cory has."

Cory groaned inwardly at this choice of words. Slade said sarcastically, "Oh, wouldn't I?"

His mother gave him a puzzled look over her shoulder, then glanced over at the young woman standing statue-still under the shimmering birch leaves. "Do you two know each other?"

"No!" said Cory.

"How could we?" Slade demanded.

Cory said, skating on the very edge of truth, "For a moment your son reminded me of someone I used to know, Mrs. Hargreave—someone I knew rather well."

"Ah," said Mrs. Hargreave. Matter-of-factly she added, "Cory, why don't you tell Slade your plans? That will give me the chance to hear them again too."

Her voice stilted, all her movements as jerky as a squirrel's, Cory described the shrubs and mulch that would make the garden both attractive and low-maintenance; Slade, she was almost sure, wasn't taking in a word she said. When she'd finished, she said, "Mrs. Hargreave, what I'll do is draw up a couple of plans along with the cost and then drop them off tomorrow afternoon."

"That would be wonderful. You won't forget a bench in the shade, will you? And I'd like a bird bath and a place for feeders in the winter."

"Some of the plantings will be specifically for attracting birds," Cory said. "And please feel free to call me with any suggestions or further questions you might have...it's a lot easier to change things at this stage than later on."

"Thank you so much," the old lady said, favoring Cory with a generous smile. Cory managed a credible smile back, gave Slade the most minimal of nods and hurried round the side of the house to the street. Her car was parked nearby. She ran across the road and scrambled into the driver's seat, desperate to get as far from Slade as she could.

On the way back to her office, she checked on the progress of a garden in the south end, and was pleased to see that the two horticultural students she'd hired for

the summer were working extremely well together. There
were two messages waiting for her at the office, both of
which she answered with an efficiency that at some level
amazed her. She then headed home.

After locking the front door behind her with the same
urgency as an army pulling up the drawbridge against
the enemy, Cory sat down hard at the kitchen table.
Slade's mother lived in Halifax. She, Cory, was carrying
the grandchild of a woman she had only met that
morning, whom she had warmed to immediately, and
who was a potential long-term customer.

This hadn't been in the bargain. Far from it.

Why hadn't Slade *told* her?

Furthermore, she realized with a lurch of her stomach,
Slade obviously visited Halifax to see his mother: he was
here now. He hadn't told her that, either.

Shock was wearing off, to be replaced by an anger
both intense and invigorating. While it would have been
all too easy to pace up and down the kitchen floor for
the next hour, muttering imprecations under her breath,
this was Cory's busiest time of year, during which she
made the bulk of her income.

She ate a sandwich and drank a glass of skimmed milk,
went upstairs, turned on the computer and forced herself
to concentrate. She'd work on the plans for Mrs.
Hargreave first. That way they'd be done and she could
maybe—just maybe—put the old lady out of her mind.

The three-dimensional mock-ups had just emerged
from the printer and Cory was typing up the estimates
when the doorbell rang. A prolonged ring. As if the
person outside was extremely impatient to get in.

She turned off the computer, walked down the stairs
with some of the deliberation of Mary Queen of Scots
going to her execution, and was not at all surprised when
she saw Slade standing on the step. She unlocked then

opened the door. "Come in," she said coolly. "I thought it might be you."

He slammed the door shut behind him and said savagely, "What the hell do you think you're doing trying to get my mother as a customer? Are you out of your mind?"

"I didn't know she was your mother!"

"Come off it. If you researched me as thoroughly as you said you did, you knew her name. My stepfather was a well-known collector of Canadian first editions—he's nearly always mentioned in articles about me."

She glared at him. "Are you calling me a liar?"

"I don't believe in coincidence," he said shortly.

"It *was* coincidence. She got me in for her birthday and that's why you're here too. Anyway, why would I be cultivating the acquaintance of your mother?"

"Despite that little bungalow, she's a very wealthy woman."

"Oh, this is just lovely," Cory jeered. "The father of my child thinks I'm avaricious, dishonest and sneaky. You wonder why I don't want to get married? Men like you is why."

"Don't you put me in the same boat with your—"

"Until you walked into that garden," Cory interrupted furiously, "Mrs. Lavinia Hargreave was just a potential customer who phoned me a couple of days ago to ask for an estimate. And if we're into throwing accusations at each other, why didn't you *tell* me you had a mother in Halifax? Slade, I'm carrying her grandchild, for heaven's sake!"

As though her words had evoked it, to her utter horror she felt sickness well up in her throat. With an incoherent gasp of dismay she ran for the downstairs bathroom, slamming the door behind her.

Slade, left alone, tried to organize his thoughts into some kind of order for the first time since he'd walked out into the sunshine in his mother's garden and seen Cory standing beneath the birch tree. Her presence, so unexpected, her beauty, so well remembered, had ripped through him as ruthlessly as a scythe through grass; all he could think was that somehow she had planned this meeting, that she was using his mother for purposes of her own.

Where was she now? What was wrong?

He hurried down the hallway, calling her name. She'd gone as white as a sheet and run away from him as though a pack of rabid dogs were pursuing her. "Cory?" he called again.

From behind a closed door Slade heard the sound of running water. He tapped on the door. "Are you all right?"

"No! Go away."

"What's the matter?"

"Slade," Cory choked, "will you please leave?"

Deliberately he opened the door. She was hunched over the basin. She was as white as a sheet. Add bruised blue shadows under her eyes and an expression of utter misery and you had the whole picture, he thought. "What's the matter?" he repeated.

She sloshed cold water over her face. "Morning sickness. Except that with me it's all-afternoon-and-often-well-into-the-evening sickness and I truly hate it. In my next incarnation I'm going to be a man."

Not if he could help it, thought Slade, and decided not to share this particular sentiment with her; she didn't look as though she'd be very receptive. Janie, his wife, had never let him see any of the inconveniences and difficulties of pregnancy; she'd been almost pathologically private about her body. Feeling helpless and awkward, he said, "Is there anything I can do?"

"Go away!" she wailed, and bent over the basin again.

Her braid had fallen over her shoulder, exposing her nape. With a hesitation that was uncharacteristic of him, Slade took her by the shoulders. She seemed thinner than she'd been two months ago; as she was racked by another bout of sickness, he held her more tightly, murmuring meaningless words of comfort. When she finally sagged in his hold, he dampened the edge of the nearest towel, turned her in his arms and wiped her face. It was streaked with involuntary tears and her smile was wobbly.

"Not much fun," he said.

"The trouble is that smack-dab in the middle of it I get cravings for things like cherry-swirl ice cream and pickled beets."

Chuckling, he drew her to his chest, smoothing her hair with one hand and content just to hold her. "You've lost weight."

"Nothing stays down." She raised her head and added quickly, "But I'm eating all the right things and drinking lots of milk."

"Cory," he said gently, "I know you'll do the best you can for this baby."

The expression on his face filled Cory with an inappropriate mixture of pain and desire. "I need to clean my teeth," she muttered, and pulled free of him.

She brushed them strenuously and gargled with mouthwash. When she finally looked up, Slade met her eyes in the mirror and said, "You didn't know she was my mother, did you?"

"No. I already told you I have a predilection for the truth."

The little girl shut in the closet. "Then I owe you an apology, Cory—I'm sorry." Knowing he was speaking the truth, he said, "I don't think there's an avaricious bone in your body."

Cory bit her lip. "I wish you'd told me about her— I would never have taken her on as a client."

"When she moved in, she said she wasn't going to bother with a garden. So it didn't occur to me that you'd meet."

"Oh, well...once I begin to show, I'll send Dillon instead."

Involuntarily his eyes dropped to her waist and the flatness of her belly. "I still want to take you to bed," he said in a raw voice. "That hasn't changed."

I'd still go with you.

For a moment Cory thought she'd said the words out loud. She might just as well have; swift comprehension flashed across Slade's features. Before she could think of a word to say, he cupped her face in his palms and kissed her deeply and passionately.

She felt like a snowdrop warmed by the first rays of the spring sun, like a wilting flower drinking in water after a long drought. She wound her arms around his neck and kissed him back, fiercely and hungrily, for how could the flower deny its need for water?

Slade swung her up into his arms and edged his way out into the hall. As he carried her up the stairs, she undid the top buttons of his shirt, playing with the tangled hair on his chest. Halfway up he stopped to kiss her again, a long, drugged kiss that made his heart pound in his chest. Dimly, in the back of his mind, the thought surfaced that he was carrying the whole world in his arms; woman and child. His, both of them.

This time he knew the way to her room. He laid her on the bed and fell on top of her, kissing her as though there were no tomorrow, fumbling with the buttons on her shirt. With frantic haste and in utter silence they discarded their clothes. Her breasts were fuller than he remembered and her skin had a translucence that aroused in him a dual and powerful need: to possess her and to protect her. The protection, he thought, was something new.

That she had once felt shy with him seemed impossible to Cory. She whispered, "You're so familiar to me, Slade. I don't think I've forgotten one thing we— Oh, yes, please, there... and there."

"You don't know how I've longed for this," he muttered, his hands roaming her body. "Night after night I've woken wanting you." Inflamed by her boldness, he pulled her on top of him, glorying in her weight, in the dark shine of her eyes and the swollen softness of her lips as she hovered over him, moving against his groin with a mingled seduction and innocence that touched him to the core.

When he entered her, she was more than ready for him. He let himself be drawn deeper and deeper into her body, watching the storm gather in her eyes and waiting for her first, fierce cry before his own tumultuous release claimed him. Then he circled her in his arms, one thigh lying heavy over hers, and lay still. She smiled at him drowsily. "I feel wonderful. This is a lot better than cherry-swirl ice cream."

"And pickled beets too, I hope."

She ran her finger down his cheek. "You look tired. And you've lost weight, too."

Not for anything was he going to tell her that ever since he'd found out she was pregnant all the old nightmares had returned, the ones that had haunted his sleep after the accident; during the previous few months he'd been more or less free of them. "Lifting weights and playing squash," he said. "In theory as a curb to lust."

"You mean it doesn't work?" she asked, wide-eyed.

"Couldn't you tell?"

She blushed, then gave a wide yawn. "The other thing I keep doing—besides losing my lunch—is falling asleep."

"Then maybe we should get under the covers instead of on top of them," he suggested. Two minutes later she was sound asleep in his arms. Happiness, he decided, was Cory's arm draped over his chest, her cheek cuddled into his shoulder.

Nothing very complicated about that.

Was there?

Slade woke an hour later to the shrill of the phone beside the bed. Cory sat up, rubbing at her eyes, and grabbed the receiver. "Hello?" she gasped. "Hi, Dillon, what's up? They *what*? All afternoon? The idiots; don't they have an ounce of common sense? OK. I'll be there in fifteen minutes."

As she scrambled off the bed she said, "A special order of ornamental grasses from Ontario was left baking in the sun all afternoon; I'll have to go and help Dillon... Dammit, where's my other sock?"

Slade leaned on his elbow, watching her breasts jiggle as she pulled on her shorts. "I could help too."

Cory didn't want Dillon and Slade within fifty feet of each other; Dillon was making no secret of the fact that the father of this baby should, in his opinion, be on hand day and night. She hauled her shirt on, somehow managed to get the buttons in the right buttonholes, and located her sock on top of the bureau; she had no idea how it had landed there. She laced up her sneakers and stood up.

The sheets were swathed around Slade's hips; dark hair arrowed to his navel in a way that entranced her. She loved everything about his body, she thought helplessly, and blurted, "How did we end up here?"

"Because we both wanted to."

She could scarcely argue with that. "It shouldn't have happened. It's not in the plan."

"Cory," Slade said in a hard voice, "if you're frightened or confused or upset, just say so. But don't dump on a lovemaking that was—'' He sought for the right word to express that earth-shattering sense of union.

''Elemental,'' she supplied in a small voice.

Their eyes met in a long exchange which acknowledged the overwhelming intimacy they had shared, as well as its inevitable climax. Slade said harshly, ''You'd better go and tend to business. Or you'll have dead ornamental grasses, not live ones.''

She made a gesture of total confusion. ''When I got up this morning, I never thought anything like this would happen today.'' And, she thought, unable to be anything but honest with herself, I'd do it again. Right now. Me, who hated going to bed with Rick. ''Slade,'' she finished desperately, ''I've got to go—will you let yourself out? Push in the doorhandle to lock it.''

''Sure,'' he said, and added prosaically, ''Take care.''

Neither of them, noticeably, said anything about another meeting. But when Cory got home at about seven, having rescued and resuscitated the plants, she found a brown paper bag sitting on the sill of her front door. In it was a bottle of pickled beets.

Slade both loved and liked his mother, a rarer combination than might be supposed. But all evening, as they ate dinner then went for a stroll along the shaded streets, Cory's words were ringing in his head. ''I'm carrying her grandchild...'' she'd said. The grandchild his mother wanted.

Lavinia was both proud and reticent, and would probably never mention the matter again. But this was a woman whose first marriage had been far from happy, and who had borne the grief of her second husband's death with courage and dignity. How could he deprive her of something so elemental—his mind winced from the word—as a grandchild?

Yet that was precisely what he was doing.

He went to bed early, closing the door to his room and flinging himself down on the comfortable three-quarter-size bed. What was Cory doing right now? Was she in bed too? In the bed where in the middle of a summer afternoon he'd found fulfillment beyond anything he'd ever known?

Janie, no matter how gentle he'd been or how carefully he'd masked his body's needs, had always seemed a little frightened of him, or perhaps of the act of sex itself. She'd never once, in the eight years of their marriage, embraced him with Cory's fervor or laughed with Cory's unabashed and astounded delight; as a direct consequence, he'd never behaved with Janie as freely or as tempestuously as he had with Cory.

He must have failed Janie in some basic way and without in the least wanting to; he was still convinced of that. And he found this failure painful, adding it to the burden of guilt and grief he'd carried ever since she and Rebecca had died.

Rebecca . . . his daughter.

He pounded his pillow, turned out the bedside light and surprisingly fell asleep immediately. But at two in the morning he woke to the echo of his own hoarse cry and to the racing of his heart, his brain seared by the nightmare images of a dream that over time had carved itself into his consciousness.

He'd made the mistake of seeing the van after the accident, so that twisted steel and shattered glass were part of the dream. Blood-red was the predominant color of the dream. But worst of all were the screams, Janie's and Rebecca's, a terrible mingling of sounds that made his chest ache with a long-held agony and his eyes sting with tears.

He sat up in bed, running his fingers through his hair, knowing from experience that it was useless to try and sleep again until he'd calmed down. At home in his

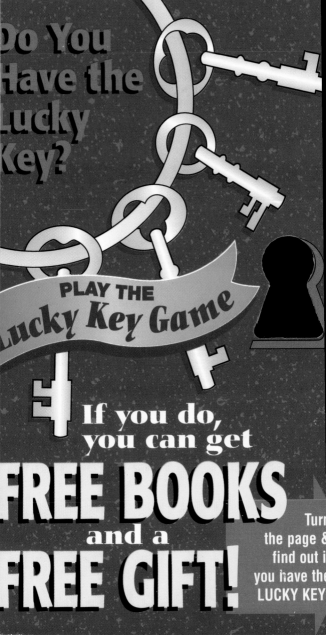

PLAY THE
Lucky Key Game
and ge

HOW TO PLAY:

1. With a coin, carefully scratch off gold area at the right. Then check the claim chart to s what we have for you — **FREE BOOKS** and a **FREE GIFT** — **ALL YOURS FREE!**

2. Send back this card and you'll receive brand-new Harlequin Presents® novels. These books have a cover price of $3.75 each, but they are yours to keep absolutely free.

3. There's no catch. You're under no obligation to buy anything. We charge nothing — ZERO — for your first shipment. And you don't have to make any minimum number purchases — not even one!

4. The fact is thousands of readers enjoy receiving books by mail from the Harlequin Reader Service® months before they're available in stores. They like the convenience of home delivery and they love our discount prices!

5. We hope that after receiving your free books you'll want to remain a subscriber. But the choice is yours — to continu or cancel, any time at all! So why not take us up on our invitation, with no risk of any kind. You'll be glad you did!

YOURS FREE!
A SURPRISE MYSTERY GIFT

We can't tell you what it is...but we're sure you'll like it! A
FREE GIFT—
just for playing the LUCKY KEY game!

FREE GIFTS!

NO COST! NO OBLIGATION TO BUY!
NO PURCHASE NECESSARY!

PLAY THE
Lucky Key Game

Scratch gold area with a coin.
Then check below to see the gifts you get!

YES! I have scratched off the gold area. Please send me all the gifts for which I qualify. I understand I am under no obligation to purchase any books, as explained on the back and on the opposite page.

106 HDL CH77

Name _____
(PLEASE PRINT CLEARLY)
Address _____ Apt.# _____

City _____ State _____ Zip _____

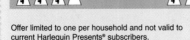

2 free books plus a mystery gift	1 free book
2 free books	Try Again!

DETACH AND MAIL CARD TODAY!

The Harlequin Reader Service™ — Here's how it works:

Accepting free books places you under no obligation to buy anything. You may keep the books and gift and return the shipping statement marked "cancel." If you do not cancel, about a month later we'll send you 6 additional novels and bill you just $3.12 each, plus 25¢ delivery per book and applicable sales tax, if any.* That's the complete price — and compared to cover prices of $3.75 each — quite a bargain! You may cancel at any time, but if you choose to continue, every month we'll send you 6 more books, which you may either purchase at the discount price...or return to us and cancel your subscription.

*Terms and prices subject to change without notice. Sales tax applicable in N.Y.

If offer card is missing write to: Harlequin Reader Service, 3010 Walden Ave., P.O. Box 1867, Buffalo NY 14240-1867

BUSINESS REPLY MAIL
FIRST-CLASS MAIL   PERMIT NO. 717   BUFFALO, NY

POSTAGE WILL BE PAID BY ADDRESSEE

HARLEQUIN READER SERVICE
3010 WALDEN AVE
PO BOX 1867
BUFFALO NY 14240-9952

NO POSTAGE
NECESSARY
IF MAILED
IN THE
UNITED STATES

apartment he'd usually get up and work, or turn on the television. But here, even though his mother was a sound sleeper, he didn't want to risk disturbing her.

He was a grown man, he thought in frustration. He'd taken part in the usual teenage escapades of fast cars and skiing stunts, and in his early twenties he'd owned a Harley-Davidson and been fascinated by rock climbing. After the accident he'd gone into skydiving and hang-gliding, neither of which had managed to kill him. But nothing he'd ever done had frightened him as much as the dream did.

The message of the dream was clear, he thought, staring at the wall. He wasn't ready to risk intimacy again, not with a wife and certainly not with a child; losing Rebecca had torn the heart from his body.

He'd already been intimate with Cory at a level that had touched his soul: not all of that intimacy had been physical.

Get out now. Before it's too late, an inner voice urged. Cory Haines isn't for you. She never was.

CHAPTER EIGHT

SLADE did eventually get back to sleep. In the morning his mother was delighted with the assortment of birthday gifts he'd brought her. He joined a group of her friends for lunch, and afterwards, while she had what she rather grandly called a siesta—"only old women have afternoon naps, Slade"—he tried to involve himself in one of the latest thrillers on the bestseller list. At three-thirty the doorbell chimed.

Cory. With the plans.

But a young man stood on the step. He was wearing beige pants and a shirt with a logo that Slade recognized, even in the midst of a crushing disappointment that made nonsense of all his resolutions. He was an extremely handsome young man: blond, blue-eyed and blatantly sexual. Dillon, thought Slade. She's sent Dillon instead of coming herself.

Women must flock to Dillon in droves.

The young man said, holding out an envelope, "Please would you give this to Mrs. Hargreave? It's the garden plans from Cory—I'm her assistant."

Slade didn't like hearing Cory's name on Dillon's lips. Didn't like it at all. I'm behaving like an adolescent, he chided himself, and said, "I thought she was going to drop them off herself."

"She usually works at home in the afternoons," Dillon said vaguely. "You got any questions you can call her home number; it's on the estimate."

"I see. I'll make sure Mrs. Hargreave gets this, thanks."

Dillon walked back down the path with a swagger worthy of a cowboy. Slade went indoors, found a pad of paper and a pen and started scribbling a letter. Seven or eight versions later, he crumpled up the rejects and thrust them deep in the plastic garbage bag in the basement, and sealed the final result in a plain white envelope.

Because he'd tried to keep his feelings out of it, it sounded cold and detached. But it was the best he could do. Before he could change his mind, he borrowed his mother's car and drove to Cory's house. Her car was parked in the driveway.

What kind of a coward are you, Slade Redden? he sneered, and pounded on her door. No one answered. He knocked again, not knowing whether to be relieved or disappointed. Then the door opened.

She had the pallor of a ghost and there were circles under her eyes. "Slade!" she wailed, and threw herself at him, circling his waist and leaning her whole weight on him.

This, Cory thought muzzily, was what Sue had meant about not being alone. Slade felt as solid as the red oak tree in her next-door neighbor's garden. Heavenly.

Slade staggered a little, got his balance and put his arms round her, the letter still clutched in his left hand. "Afternoon sickness?" he said.

She moaned. "I feel the pits...I'm so glad you're here."

So was he. And the emotion flooding him was unquestionably tenderness. He said flatly, "I came to talk to you."

Cory looked up. She didn't like the tone of his voice or the look on his face. "You'd better come in," she said, and disentangled herself from an embrace that no longer felt safe.

In the living room she turned to face him, her chin well up, her brown eyes guarded, and waited for him to speak. Deliberately recalling the terror and pain that had woken him in the night, Slade said, "You've been right all along, Cory; we shouldn't be seeing each other. Nor should we—let's be honest—be making love the way we did yesterday.

"We struck a bargain, each of us for very good reasons, and I think we should stick to it. I'll get my mother to visit me in Toronto next time, and when I do come here I won't get in touch with you." He scowled. "Although I still want you to let me know when the baby's born."

It was what she'd wanted—to be left alone. Why then did she feel as though a boxer had suddenly given her a hard left hook to the side of the head? Swallowing nausea, Cory said stiffly, "You're right, of course." Then, through the ringing in her ears, she noticed the long white envelope in his hand. "What's that?"

"I'd written you a note in case you weren't here." Not for anything was he going to give it to her now. She looked terrible, he thought dispassionately. He had to get out of here. "That's really all I had to say. Except look after yourself, Cory."

"I will," she said with a meaningless smile, and followed him to the front door.

Slade knew he'd be finished if he kissed her goodbye. He let himself out and strode down the front path to his car, and didn't once look back.

Cory shut the door and leaned her forehead on its cool, varnished wood. The loneliness and hurt that had engulfed her went far beyond tears.

Slade had left her. For good. As he had every right to do.

*   *   *

Three months later, early in September, Slade flew to Halifax. The plane's flight path gave him a distant view of the city, with its harbor, its islands and its twin bridges, and he felt like telling the pilot to turn around and go back to Toronto. Cory was somewhere down there, he thought. Cory and his unborn child.

He had neither seen her nor heard from her since his last visit in June. Not that that was surprising. Nor had he been in touch.

The bargain, he thought grimly, was firmly in place.

Although his mother had wanted him to come down through the summer to see her garden, he'd put her off; but he couldn't keep on doing that without hurting her feelings. He'd make all the appropriate comments about the garden as soon as he got there, and in a couple of days he could head home again.

He wouldn't go near Cory's little Cape Cod house.

The plane landed and an hour later Slade arrived outside his mother's bungalow. He was scarcely in the door before he found out that Lavinia had tickets to a symphony concert that evening whose guest artist was a rather famous violinist. In deep distress he realized there was a very good chance that Cory would be there. It was just the sort of thing she'd go to.

"You don't mind, do you, Slade?" Lavinia asked. "Perhaps I should have told you. But I thought it would be a nice surprise."

It was a surprise all right. Slade summoned his most convincing smile. "It'll be great. I'm impressed they got someone of that caliber."

"It's given ticket sales a real boost. Dinner's nearly ready, dear; make yourself at home."

At quarter to eight Slade ushered his mother into her seat at the concert hall and sat down beside her. The air was humming with the kind of anticipation that a big name engendered; the program included the

Mendelssohn violin concerto, one of his favorites. As his mother started talking to the woman in the seat next to her, he found himself checking out as much of the audience as he could without being too obvious about it, his nerves as discordant as the sounds coming from the orchestra.

People were still arriving, the majority of the women in summer dresses; Halifax was experiencing a spell of unusually hot weather. For several minutes Slade didn't see anyone he knew, let alone Cory, and gradually he began to relax. But then, in the far aisle, a woman's burnished head caught his attention. His heart slammed against his ribcage and his fingers tensed on the glossy pages of the program. It was Cory.

A man, a stranger to Slade, was at her side. Her hand was resting on his sleeve, while he was stooping to hear something she'd just said; whatever it was, it made him laugh. They looked comfortable with each other, Slade thought savagely. As though their relationship wasn't new.

She'd had three months to build it.

She looked unmistakably pregnant.

Two people on the end of the row stood up and Cory edged into her seat. She was wearing a loose and very becoming sea-green dress. She took the man's jacket from him, then sat down and passed it to him, their two heads close together.

"Slade, this is Nancy Slaunwhite, a cousin of Wendell's—Slade?"

"Sorry," he muttered, and shook hands with the woman, her name already gone from his mind. Somehow he made conversation in a manner that must have made sense; neither Lavinia nor the woman was looking at him strangely. The dimming of the house lights came as a huge relief.

Mozart and Haydn got him to the intermission. Determined to stay put in his chair, he heard Lavinia say, "Would you mind getting us both drinks, Slade? It's awfully warm in here, isn't it? And the bar's always such a crush."

Short of resorting to rudeness, he was stuck. He traipsed up the aisle behind them, keeping his eyes dead ahead, and left them in the lobby while he joined the line-up at the bar. He'd just presented the woman—what the dickens was her name?—with a soda and his mother with a rum and Coke when to his horror he saw Cory and her escort heading right for them. Cory hadn't noticed them; she was talking animatedly to the man. She looked blooming, he thought. Pregnancy agreed with her.

Lavinia said cordially, "Why, Cory, I didn't realize you were married."

Cory's head jerked round. Appalled, she saw Slade's mother, and then Slade standing beside her. The peach flush drained from her cheeks. She gasped, "I'm not."

Lavinia was nothing if not modern in her outlook. "That was tactless of me, dear, wasn't it? After all, what's a piece of paper? I'm glad to see you looking so well. By the way, this is Nancy Slaunwhite, a cousin of my late husband's...and you remember my son Slade?"

Oh, yes, thought Cory, swallowing a hysterical urge to giggle her head off. I remember him.

Good manners impelled her to introduce her escort. Kicking him hard on the shin with her pretty high-heeled sandal, she said, "This is Ralph Brownlee."

Lavinia shook his hand. "Congratulations, Mr. Brownlee. Cory, when are you due?"

"December," Cory said. "Are you enjoying the concert?"

Subtle, Cory, really subtle. But in a scene that has all the elements of farce except that there's no curtain to end it, what else am I supposed to say? That Ralph is the husband of my best friend? That the father of my child is standing six inches to your right, Mrs. Hargreave, and just happens to be your son?

My own mother wouldn't have thought much of this.

Nancy Slaunwhite made a knowledgeable comment about the brass section, and Ralph, who loved symphonic music, picked up on it; their conversation gathered momentum. Slade said nothing.

He didn't need to, Cory thought, another hysterical giggle gathering in her throat, her gaze wincing away from his. He looked like thunder; Ralph, by rights, should have dissolved into a puddle on the floor.

But Ralph was made of sterner stuff than that. Having accepted the role of fathering Cory's child without so much as a blink of his eye, he was now serenely discussing Haydn's use of counterpoint. Mrs. Hargreave said placidly, "Are you feeling well, Cory?"

"Fine, thank you. The first three months were rough, I do have to admit that."

"I understand now why your assistant's been looking after my garden all this time—he's doing an excellent job, by the way. Two green thumbs and oodles of charm; quite a combination."

Her description of Dillon was apt. Pulling herself together, Cory asked after the New England asters and the sedum, and, as Mrs. Hargreave chatted on, was aware through every nerve in her body of the force of Slade's silence, of the closeness of his body. Her heart had stopped thrumming in her chest like a panicked bird's and had settled into a slow, heavy pounding. Like a mattock thudding into a very hard subsoil, she thought, and decided she'd had enough of Slade glowering at her. She said naughtily, "Are we boring you, Mr. Redden?"

Sparks struck from the flint of his eyes. "I'm not bored, no, Ms. Haines. Tell me, do you propose to marry the father of your child, or are you above such petty moral constraints?''

As his mother gasped at his rudeness, Cory said smoothly, ''Well, actually, he's never asked me. To marry him, I mean.''

''How remiss of him,'' said Slade. ''And would you accept were he to remedy his error?''

Score one, Slade, she thought, and wondered why she'd ever embarked on this ridiculous exchange. Fugitive laughter gleaming in her dark eyes, she countered, ''Do you think I should?''

''Off-white, so I've been told, is very fashionable this year. And family values are back in a big way.''

''I've always looked good in beige,'' Cory said demurely. ''But I don't think I'll hold my breath until I'm asked.''

''Life,'' said Slade, ''is full of surprises.''

Not the least of which is seeing you here, thought Cory, and felt Ralph nudge her with his elbow. ''I'd better take you back to your seat, hon,'' he said. ''It's even warmer out here in the lobby than it was inside. Nice meeting all of you.''

''Enjoy the rest of the concert,'' Cory said, smiling at Mrs. Hargreave and letting the same smile slide over the dark-haired man at her side. ''Goodbye.''

Ralph steered her in the direction of the left-hand door, and when they were out of earshot of Slade and his mother said testily, ''My last name is not Brownlee. It's Blackston. And I've never been unfaithful to Sue in my life—let alone with her best friend. That tall guy, the one who was looking at me as though I were a slug or an earwig only fit to be squashed and he was the one who'd take great delight in doing the deed, he's the father, isn't he?''

''You mustn't tell anyone, Ralph,'' she said frantically.

"I'll tell Sue because I tell her everything. And I don't appreciate you as good as saying to that guy that I'd never ask you to marry me. I happen to agree with Sue— leaving out the obvious factors like violence and abuse, it's better for kids if marriage and parenting go hand in hand. I think you and that Slade fellow should look very carefully at the choices you're making."

Ralph, normally mild of temper, looked markedly upset.

"I didn't know what else to do!" Cory sputtered. "His mother was standing right there, for heaven's sake."

"Right. I hope that makes *you* feel like an earwig."

Cory gave the couple at the end of the row a fake smile and eased between the seats. "I should never have come with you. But he was the last person I was expecting to see."

"You're not planting petunias here, Cory. This is a child's future we're talking about."

"I get the message," Cory said irritably, and snapped open her program, flipping through the pages until she found the notes for the Mendelssohn concerto.

Was Ralph right? Were she and Slade between them denying something all-important to a baby towards whom she already felt ferociously protective?

Whom I love, she confessed to herself. A kind of love I've never felt before.

But the question was rhetorical. Slade had no intention of asking her to marry him. Whether she wore white, off-white, beige or purple.

Slade spent the next morning up a ladder cleaning the rain gutters around his mother's house. Physical activity—especially if it took place high up, he thought with the first touch of humor since Ralph Brownlee had put his arm round Cory's waist and led her away—

usually made him feel better. This morning it wasn't working. He was furious with Cory. Livid.

How dared she get involved with Ralph Brownlee when she was carrying *his* child? How *dared* she?

This afternoon he was going to get some answers, he decided grimly, dumping the remains of a starling's nest on the ground, climbing down the ladder and moving it over four feet. Straight answers.

At two o'clock he went to Cory's house. Her car wasn't there, but he knocked loudly on the front door several times before concluding that she wasn't there either. He drove to her office, watching the tarmac shimmer in the heat and feeling his shirt stick to his back. Haines Landscaping occupied an unpretentious building on a side street in the north end; but it was newly painted and the garden in front of it was bright with annuals. A truck bearing the company logo was parked on the street.

She's here, he thought, and marched in the door. The little business office, which was immaculately tidy, was empty. But an automatic buzzer had sounded when he'd pushed open the door, and a man's voice called, "Be right there."

Dillon came in from the shed, wearing cropped jeans and a mud-stained shirt. "Can I help you, sir?"

"I'm looking for Cory," Slade said without finesse.

"She's not here right now. Is there anything I can do?"

"Where can I find her?"

Slade's tone was peremptory and he hadn't bothered to smile. Dillon said thoughtfully, "If you have a complaint, I can probably—"

"No, thanks. I want to talk to her. Just her."

Dillon's deep blue eyes narrowed. "She might still be at the Dow Street project. I can give you directions—"

But Slade had already turned away. "I know where it is," he said.

"Are you Slade Redden by any chance?" Dillon rapped, his voice no more friendly than Slade's.

"Yes," said Slade, one hand on the door.

"You donated the Dow Street site and the one on Cornell."

"That's right," Slade said impatiently. "Excuse me, I want to catch Cory before—"

"Are you by any chance the jerk who got her pregnant?" Dillon said belligerently, coming round the end of the counter.

Slade dropped the doorhandle. You want a fight, Dillon, you'll get one, he thought, and said evenly, "Yeah . . . not that it's anything to do with you."

"Got her pregnant then hightailed it back to Toronto. Was taking her to bed part of the deal? Sorry, Cory, no land unless you lie flat on your back?"

His eyes savage, Slade spat, "No!" Then he took a deep breath and slowly unclenched his fists. "I don't operate that way."

"Could've fooled me." Dillon's scowl deepened. "I remember now . . . you were at Mrs. Hargreave's the day I dropped off the estimate. That's three months ago, and I haven't seen you rushing to help Cory out in the meantime."

"Has it occurred to you that Cory might not want help?"

"No, as a matter of fact it hasn't," Dillon drawled. "Right after I met you that first time, I saw her crying in here—crying enough to water the whole damn garden, and she happens to be my friend as well as my boss. We got a name for creeps like you where I come from."

"Dillon," Slade said tightly, "if you're spoiling for a fight, so am I. But I don't think Cory would appreciate either one of us starting a brawl in her office. Let me tell you something—it was her idea to get pregnant."

Dillon gave a rude laugh, and in a string of swearwords of impressive virtuosity managed to insult both Slade's manhood and his mother. Moving so fast that Dillon didn't have time to evade him, Slade lifted the younger man off his feet, thrust him back against the counter and snarled, "Your boss is driving me out of my mind and I'm on my way to try and talk some sense into her—instead of trying to stop me, you should be wishing me luck. Luck I'll need because she's got to be the most pigheaded woman I've ever come across. As for this famous pregnancy, it was her idea. You can believe me or not—I really don't give a hoot in hell!"

He dropped Dillon without ceremony and was out the door before the other man could say anything. But his last glimpse of Dillon was of him standing very still with that same thoughtful look on his face. Dillon, unfortunately, wasn't stupid.

Going to bed with Cory Haines was the dumbest thing he, Slade, had ever done.

CHAPTER NINE

SLADE drove to Dow Street as fast as he could, parked a block away and walked towards the site. When he got there, even though his first instinct was to look for Cory and he was in a foul mood, he felt his steps slow and a smile of surprised pleasure tug at his mouth.

Instead of the bleak deserted lot he'd seen in March, there were now neat rows of garden plots, marked off by strips of grass and tool sheds; sunflowers and scarlet runners swayed in the breeze, and the green globes of squash and the orange globes of pumpkins nestled among their leafy vines. A few people were bent over in the sun, gathering and weeding, while children's voices from the playground rose and fell like the cries of birds.

It was a peaceful scene and he felt proud to have been part of its creation. But most of the credit had to go to Cory. It had been her idea.

Not all her ideas were crazy, he thought wryly, and asked the nearest person, an old gentleman with neon-pink braces, if he'd seen Cory. The old gentleman leaned on his spade. "She left five . . . ten minutes ago. Ada! Where'd Cory go?"

Ada tipped back her straw sunhat, brandishing a zucchini the size of a roll of salami. "Said she was goin' home. Too hot for her, I reckon."

Not as hot as it was going to be. Slade nodded his thanks and took the shortest route to Cory's house, where this time her car was parked in the driveway. The blinds were closed in the living-room windows to keep out the heat.

But no one answered the door. As he stood there hesitating, wondering whether she was purposely avoiding him, he heard a scraping noise from behind the house. He took the flagstone path, which was edged with fragrant Rugosa roses, and walked round to the back garden. Cory was about to lift the top one of three plastic bags of earth that were piled on a wheelbarrow. He said loudly, "I'll do that—you shouldn't be lifting."

She jumped as though he'd fired off a rifle ten feet behind her and whirled to face him. "Who invited you?"

"I'm a big boy—I came all on my own," he said. "You got Ralph hidden away in the house?"

"You got a search warrant?" she countered, and bent to the top bag.

"Cory, I'll lift those," Slade repeated softly.

"They're not heavy. I can manage."

He bumped her out of the way with his hip and hoisted the first two bags. "Where do you want me to put them?"

She said sulkily, "By the rock garden. I'm going to plant more bulbs and the earth's sunk over the summer."

She watched him move the bags with as little effort as if they were full of rice puffs, not compost, trying all the while not to stare at the play of his muscles under his shirt. When he'd finished she said ungraciously, "Thank you," and waited for his next move. There was going to be one. She was certain of that.

He said pleasantly, "Do you want to fight here or in the house?"

Wishing she were wearing something a little more dignified than maternity shorts and an oversize T-shirt on which Sylvester the cat was about to pounce on the Tweety bird, Cory answered, "It's too hot to fight. Anywhere."

"Unfortunately this won't keep until the first frost," Slade said, and took her by the arm.

He had shoved his dark glasses up into his hair, which shone in the sun; his eyes looked depthless, and he was bigger than she remembered him being. It was also glaringly obvious to her just from the touch of his fingers on her elbow that she'd be more than happy to make love to him right here in the middle of the lawn. She'd never before thought of her elbow as being an erogenous zone. A whole new area of research, she thought, and announced, "We're going to stay outside."

"Then let's at least stand in the shade."

She followed him over to the ornamental crab apple, which not only protected them from the sun but also shielded them from sight of the neighbors. "If lifting's bad for me, I bet fighting is too."

"You should have thought of that five months ago. How long have you known Ralph?"

"Five years."

A muscle twitched in Slade's jaw. "Why didn't you get him to father your child?"

"It didn't occur to me," Cory said with perfect truth. "Why are you so angry, Slade?"

"You're carrying my child—I scarcely think it's the time for you to get involved with someone else."

This, Slade knew, was only part of the truth. But how could he tell her that the thought of another man bringing up his child once it was born hurt him in the same deep place where he carried the loss of Rebecca?

She said with infuriating calmness, "Are you jealous?"

"You're darn right I am."

She'd expected him to deny it. Well, if he could be honest, so too could she. With a small, secretive smile she said, "I'd have hated seeing you at the symphony with anyone other than your mother."

"You know what? I can't stand women who play off one man against another!" So that he wouldn't grab her, Slade wrapped his fingers around a branch just over his head, making the shiny red apples bob up and down. "Are you going to marry him?"

"Absolutely not."

"Right—you're not into marriage; how could I have forgotten that? When's he moving in?"

"He's not! He—"

"Have you slept with him?" Slade's nails dug into the bark.

As Cory took an angry breath, the Tweety bird flapped up and down. "You listen to me for a minute, Slade Redden! He's already married. To—"

"*Cory!* The first question you asked me five months ago was whether I was married. What's so different about this guy?"

"Will you please stop interrupting?" she said tightly, tossing her head back so her braid flipped over her shoulder. "Ralph is married to my best friend Sue. Who had a migraine last night. Which is why I was at the concert with Ralph."

His face a picture, Slade said, "Sue . . . the one who had the baby."

"That's right."

Cory had looked comfortable with Ralph because they were old friends. Not because they were lovers. In a great wash of relief Slade demanded, "Are you seeing anyone else?"

"Slade, I'm running a business that has to make most of its money in the summer, we've had a heat wave that feels like I've migrated to Brazil and I'm five months pregnant. Have a heart."

"I'm not dating anyone in Toronto either. Don't want to," he said, and added clumsily, "I think about you a lot, Cory."

Color crept up her cheeks. She said impetuously, "I'm sorry about the whole Ralph scene—if I'd known last

March all this was going to get so complicated, I'd never have started it. But what else was I supposed to do last night when your mother saw I was pregnant except kick Ralph in the shins and pray that he'd cooperate?"

"If he ever gets fired from his present job, he could go into acting," Slade said caustically.

"If it makes you feel any better, he tore a strip off me afterwards. He thinks babies should have two parents."

She was ripping one of the glossy dark red leaves into little pieces, letting them fall one by one onto the grass; she looked tired and unhappy. Slade said, "When I went to the office looking for you, Dillon said more or less the same thing—although more colorfully than Ralph, I'd be willing to bet."

"I've been doing my best to keep you and Dillon apart."

"Cory," Slade said, "why don't we go to the beach for a swim? Right now."

Her whole face lit up. "Really?" she said.

"I might even buy you a cherry-swirl ice-cream cone."

"You remembered that?"

"I remember everything we've ever said or done."

All too often she'd had to censor her own thoughts against some of the things she and Slade had done. She said primly, "I'd love to go to the beach."

Slade went to his mother's house, picked up his swimsuit and a towel, then drove back to get Cory; they then headed towards the south shore, where they stopped at a beach Cory recommended on one of the peninsulas that marked St. Margaret's Bay. The sand hot underfoot, they walked to the far end of the beach, away from the other swimmers. The breeze rustled through the grasses; plovers pecked at the seaweed and sandpipers shuttled back and forth at the very edge of the waves. Slade spread out a blanket, and shucked off his shirt and sneakers.

Cory put down her basket. She had changed into a high-waisted sundress over her swimsuit; feeling appallingly self-conscious, she fumbled with the buttons.

Slade put his sunglasses and watch into one of his sneakers and folded his cotton trousers on top of his shirt. Looking at Cory inquiringly, he said, "Coming for a swim?"

She took a step backward, chewing her lip. Altogether too much male flesh altogether too close, she thought with a touch of desperation. Flat, taut, lean male flesh. She said, "Maternity bathing suits are about as sexy as a—a hippopotamus."

"Are you saying you feel like a hippopotamus?"

"Getting there."

The wind blew a wisp of chestnut hair across her face; the corners of her mouth were drooping. Slade said gently, "Cory, you're utterly beautiful to me."

When he looked at her like that, all she wanted to do was cry. Or kiss him senseless. "But I'm losing my figure." She gulped.

"You don't have to look like an ad in a glossy magazine all the time. You just have to be you." Reaching over, he undid the five shiny red buttons at the front of her dress and lifted it over her head. Taking his time, he let his eyes wander over her. Her swimsuit was a vivid print of turquoise, purple and green; her breasts were fuller, her cleavage deeper, and the swell of her belly filled him with such a surge of possessiveness that for a moment the sand rocked beneath his feet.

Leaning over, he kissed her, not knowing how else to express what he was feeling, and with passionate gratitude felt her hands slide up his shoulders and bury themselves in his hair even as her lips, soft and warm, moved against his. From deep within him the words formed themselves, as simple and perfect as a brier rose: I love you, he thought. Cory, I love you.

This time it was as though his whole world shifted. In sudden fear he lifted his head, and heard her murmur, "Slade, what's wrong?"

He couldn't tell her. Not yet. Not when he had no idea whether he had the courage to let those three small words change his life. Or even if he meant them. He said—and it was, as far as it went, the truth—"One kiss from you and I need a swim in the cold Atlantic."

She grinned. "I know the feeling. Let's go."

Hand in hand they waded into the waves. The spray against her skin made Cory feel tinglingly alive and she had always loved to swim. She fell forward into the translucent green curve of the next wave, surfaced and yelled, "Last one in's a chicken."

Slade splashed her with the flat of his hand and plunged after her, emerging as sleek as a seal at her side. "Tell me this was a good idea."

"You win first prize," she said. Recklessly she looped her arms around his neck and kissed him, thrusting with her tongue.

A wave submerged them both in sparkling foam. Sputtering, Cory struck out for deeper water, Slade doing a lazily proficient crawl at her side. They rode the waves, dove for shells and laughed like a couple of kids for the best part of an hour.

Their feet sinking in the sand, they then walked back to the blanket. Cory scrubbed herself dry, her eyes dancing. "I feel like a million dollars," she said, and bent and extracted from her basket two bottles of fruit punch and a large bag of chips. Sitting cross-legged on the blanket, she tipped her head back and took a long drink.

Slade stretched out on his side beside her. Her thighs were covered in goose bumps; there was a small white scar on her knee. "What happened there?" he asked idly, tearing open the chips.

"Fell off my bike when I was nine."

The wet fabric clinging to her body; his hands stilled as the crest of her belly moved, protruding then subsiding. He said in a strangled voice, "Cory..."

There was something in his face that for Cory erased all the terms of their bargain and the distance those terms were meant to enforce. She reached over and rested Slade's left hand on her swimsuit, feeling the baby kick again. She said quietly, "That's your son, Slade."

"My son?" he whispered.

"I had an ultrasound two weeks ago."

He closed his eyes, the fabric cool to his fingertips, the baby's erratic movements leveling all the defenses he'd so painstakingly constructed in the last two years. Dropping his forehead to her breast, he felt tears scald his lids.

Flooded by emotions as chaotic as the waves' tumbled foam, Cory rested her hands on his head, where the wet curls were as dark as night. It's not just the baby that's growing, she thought confusedly. Every time Slade and I get together, and in spite of both of us, something happens. I can't shrug it off any more than I can define it or prevent it.

I never meant to tell him about the ultrasound.

I never meant to see him again. Which is the biggest joke of the century.

"Are you OK?" she said softly, playing with his hair.

When he raised his head his eyes were brilliant with unshed tears, and the web that she had once spoken of entangled itself round her heart with yet another of its tensile, unbreakable strands. Slade said huskily, "Thanks for telling me, Cory."

"The doctor said that everything's fine and we're both flourishing."

"Are you happy it's a boy?"

"A healthy baby's all I want." Her brow furrowed. "But I suppose, as a single mother, a little girl might have been easier for me to handle."

He pulled away from her and said restlessly, "Dillon and Ralph both think you and I should get married."

"I'm sure your mother would feel the same way."

"But you don't."

She took a handful of chips and crunched them between her teeth. "I swore after Rick left I'd never get married again."

"So how would I go about changing your mind?"

His use of the conditional tense, she decided thoughtfully, was revealing. "You're not convinced that's what you'll do."

"So let's hypothesize."

"I can't, not about Rick," she said sharply. "It hurt too much when I realized he loved my money more than he loved me, and it was much too difficult getting rid of him."

It was the first hint she'd given him about the breakup of her marriage. "Do I remind you of him?"

"Do you think I'd have had anything to do with you if you did?"

"I thought I was the one asking the questions, Cory."

"You do not remind me of Rick," she snapped.

"Well, that's a start," Slade said affably, and opened his bottle of juice.

For some reason Cory felt extremely angry. She discovered within herself a strong curiosity to know why Slade wasn't proposing marriage on the spot, and a perverse refusal to indulge that curiosity. She said fretfully, "I shouldn't be eating chips; all that salt—I'm going for another swim," and she scrambled to her feet.

Slade watched her march into the water. A son, he thought. Cory is the mother of my son. Cory, whose moods are as mercurial as the sea. Do I love her? And if I do, what am I going to do about it?

Take her out to dinner for starters, he thought, and absently finished off the chips. When Cory came back from her swim, he said, "We're going for dinner at Tancred's—they have an outdoor patio and the best Caesar salad in town. And we're going to talk about anything under the sun except pregnancy and marriage. How about it?"

His long body was gilded by the sun and his smile was irresistible. "An early dinner," she said. "I've got to go over my books tonight; my accountant's having a fit because I'm three days late."

"I'll have you home by eight-thirty."

"I'd love to," said Cory.

Slade stood up, her towel draped over his arm. "Hold still," he said, and started wiping the drops of salt water from her skin with lazy, sensual strokes.

"I'll tell you one thing and then I swear I won't mention the word again," Cory pronounced. "Pregnancy does not reduce the libido."

Slade laughed, smoothing the towel over her cleavage and watching her irises shine with desire. "You could always tell your accountant you had an urgent appointment. In bed."

"He has no sense of humor," she said limpidly, and ran her fingernail down Slade's chest from his breastbone to his navel.

"Stop it. You're not allowed to make love in public in Nova Scotia; it's against the law."

"Lawyers have no sense of humor, either."

They drove home in high spirits. Cory took the downstairs bathroom for her shower and sent Slade upstairs. As he was crossing the hall, he looked into her bedroom, smiling involuntarily because he was quite sure they'd end up in there at some point this evening, accountant or no accountant; he then glanced into the room across from it.

His smile vanished.

Cory was setting it up as a nursery. He walked in, smelling the faint odor of the new paint on the walls, a pretty pale yellow paint. She'd added a wallpaper border of Disney characters and curtains made from a matching material. The crib, he saw with a lurch of his heart, was the exact same model as Rebecca's.

In four months' time he'd have a son. There was nothing he could do to stop the process. And then he'd be vulnerable again, vulnerable to the kind of heart-break his little daughter had brought him.

He should be taking the first plane back to Toronto. Not going out for dinner with Cory. He marched into the bathroom, locked the door and turned on the shower as hot as he could bear it, tapering it to cold before he got out. Once he was dressed, he ran downstairs to see if he could borrow a comb.

The television was on in the living room. Cory was leaning against the kitchen door drying her hair and watching the six o'clock news; her cotton shift had the same bright hues as her swimsuit and her hair wafted in a bright cloud around her head. Slade said tersely, "May I borrow your brush when you're finished?"

"Sure." She fluttered her lashes at him. "I'll dry your hair if you like."

The first plane out of here? Who was he kidding? Then her eyes flicked back to the screen and she made a tiny sound of distress; automatically he looked too. There'd been a three-car pileup on the TransCanada highway; the camera had filmed the wreckage, the ambulances, the police cars and bystanders with an impartial eye. His breath trapped somewhere in his throat, Slade felt all the color drain from his face.

Janie had been at the wheel of his new blue van that fateful day early in February. If he hadn't been so busy at work, he'd have been driving. Maybe he'd have been able to avoid the eighteen-wheeler when its brakes had failed on the hill. He'd been a better driver than Janie.

"Slade, what's the matter? Slade, don't look like that!"

By an actual physical effort he dragged himself back to the present, to the distraught woman clinging to his arm. It was Cory, he thought dazedly. Not Janie. Janie was dead.

With a sob of relief that he'd returned from whatever nightmare had claimed him, Cory said, "What happened? Please, you've got to tell me."

She had switched off the television, Slade noticed with a faraway part of his brain. He said rapidly, before he could lose his nerve, "My wife and my three-year-old daughter were killed in a car accident. Two and a half years ago. The brakes failed on a transport truck. I was at the office when it happened." What else was there to say? Everything and nothing, he thought numbly, and wished he were anywhere but in this room with this woman.

Cory faltered, "Th-that's why you don't want to get married again. Isn't it?" As he nodded, her brain made the next leap. "And why you agreed to the pregnancy."

"Not one of my brighter moves," he said, lifting her hand from his arm and prowling over to the window. "I thought if you bore my child I'd know that that child was out there in the world and being well looked after, without me having to get involved." With a bitterness that he could taste on his tongue he added, "When it comes to emotional stuff, I'm at the kindergarten level. As you may have noticed."

"Slade," Cory said steadily, "you're a struggling human being. Just like the rest of us."

"Oh, sure."

He'd turned to face her, his features in shadow because the light was at his back. Hating the dismissiveness in his voice, she went on the attack. "No one stuck at the preschool level could have made love to me the way you did. When we were in bed together you looked after me—you made me feel safe, you freed me to be myself. You were sensitive and passionate; you made me laugh and you made me cry. Don't tell me that doesn't take emotional maturity."

Slade thrust his hands in his pockets. Janie hadn't wanted those gifts of his body, and so for her sake, because he'd loved her, he'd subdued them. Cory was the very opposite, evoking in him a depth of passion he hadn't known was his. With a shudder of mingled revulsion and fear he said roughly, "We'd better go. Or you won't have the time to do your books."

She stamped her foot. "Damn the books!"

"Cory," he said, knowing the answer before he spoke, "will you marry me?"

With unconscious drama she pressed her hands to her breast, her eyes as frightened as a startled deer's. "I can't! I can't, Slade—you know that."

"Then there's no point in this discussion. Let's go eat. I'll tell you the plot of every single movie I've seen in the past three months—but I won't talk about babies and I won't talk about marriage."

Nor did they. At twenty past eight Slade walked Cory to her front door, standing back as she unlocked it. "Will you come in?" she said formally and with no real warmth.

"No, thanks; I'll let you get at your books." He hesitated. "I'll probably go back to Toronto tomorrow. Take care of yourself, won't you, Cory?"

She gave him a bright smile. "Oh, yes. You too."

"Goodbye," he said, and walked away from her to the car.

He'd made no attempt to kiss her, and all through a dinner that to her overstretched nerves had seemed to last for five hours rather than two he'd been excruciatingly polite, as if they were a couple of chance-met strangers.

After that horrible scene on the news, he'd retreated. Gone somewhere where she wasn't welcome. And how she hated it!

How was that for inconsistency? thought Cory, letting herself into the house. Talk about double messages. Oh, no, Slade, I can't marry you. Oh, yes, Slade, pour out your guts about your wife and your little daughter. Oh, no, Slade, I'm going to be a single mother. Oh, yes, Slade, you can take me to bed any time you like and the more intimate we are the better.

I'm a bundle of contradictions, she admitted to herself. Part of me wants him back in Toronto on the first plane, and the other part wants him right here right now.

"Go back to Toronto, Slade Redden," she said out loud to the empty living room. "See if I care."

After which rather childish speech she hauled out the books and did her best to deal with columns of credits and debits that seemed determined not to balance.

It wasn't until Cory went to bed and was lying alone in the darkness that she acknowledged something that she'd been doing her very best to ignore. The way Slade had said goodbye had had a horrible finality to it.

One short word with only two syllables. Yet it had cut like a knife through all the intimacy, anger and laughter they'd shared. Had he intended it as an ending, permanently separating her from him, him from her?

What if she never saw him again? How would that feel?

CHAPTER TEN

SLADE flew back to Toronto feeling something akin to peace for the first time since he'd met Cory. He'd made a decision. Despite having asked her, he wasn't going to marry Cory; furthermore, he was going to stay away from her. Permanently.

He made a flying trip to the Montreal project, dealt with some complications with an impressive blend of efficiency and imagination, and had a meeting in Calgary that promised more contracts than he'd know what to do with. And all the while he was feeling self-congratulatory about having extricated himself from the quagmire of confusion that went by the name of Cory Haines.

A week after he'd left Halifax he played squash with Bruno, one of his regular partners and one of the friends who'd helped him get through the days and months after the accident. Slade was whistling cheerfully as he strode down the corridor to the court and he slapped Bruno on the shoulder as he entered. "Watch it, fella—I've got energy to burn today."

Bruno, a giant of a man who played an erratic but never dull game, grinned at him through the thicket of his red beard. "Hey, you look better than you've looked for months. Let me guess—you've met a woman. About time."

Taken unawares, Slade said, "You've got it wrong. I've just ended a relationship with a woman."

Kneading the ball in a hand like a small ham, Bruno said genially, "What happened? She get too close for comfort?"

"I'm not ready for commitment, Bruno."

"And when do you plan to be ready?"

Bouncing lightly on the balls of his feet, Slade said irritably, "How do I know?"

"You can run around the edges of the court for the rest of your life, or you can take control of the T," Bruno said. "Time you figured out your strategy."

"I came here to play squash, buddy, not to listen to a lecture on my social life."

"I'm not talking about your social life. I'm talking about your life. Life with a capital L. You want to end up like Crenshaw?"

Crenshaw was a crabby old bachelor who organized the tournaments and terrorized the board of directors. "For Pete's sake, Bruno!"

"I don't reckon Crenshaw planned on ending up the way he did—it likely just sort of happened to him, and now he's too old to change." Bruno gave Slade an ingenuous grin. "Rally for serve?"

Five minutes into the game Slade was running for his life. His life with a small l, he thought, extricating the ball from the back corner and slamming it off the side wall. Bruno was playing with an aggression that was unusual for him, planting his large feet at the T and dominating it with a single-minded focus that was also rare.

Bruno steadied himself for the serve. "What was she like, this woman you broke up with?"

Panting, Slade said, "Hair like spun copper, eyes like velvet and a body to die for."

"There's hope," said Bruno, and thwacked the ball just above the cut line.

Slade won the rally. As he was loping to the box, Bruno asked with genuine interest, "Was she good in bed?"

"Yeah," said Slade. "Lay off, Bruno."

"She out for a wedding ring; that the problem?"

"She was not," Slade said more emphatically than was wise.

"Drink too much? Smoke cigars? Bitchy in the mornings?"

"None of those."

"Then why'd you break up? Beautiful, independent and a good lay—sounds like the single man's dream."

Slade didn't like hearing Cory described as "a good lay". "None of your business," he grated, and sliced a vicious serve straight at Bruno's massive chest.

Bruno made a wild swipe and miraculously hit the ball so low to the floor that Slade missed the return shot. "My serve," Bruno said complacently. "What's her name? Where does she live?"

Slade growled, "You're not going to quit, are you?"

"Nope. Serena and me, we're worried about you. Have been for quite a while."

Serena was Bruno's Italian wife, whose nature was anything but serene; Slade liked her very much. And he owed Bruno a debt of gratitude that he could never repay for having stuck with him so tenaciously in the dreadful aftermath of the accident. He said, his chest heaving under his sweat-soaked shirt, "Her name's Cory, she lives in Halifax, and she's nearly six months pregnant."

Bruno dropped his racquet and his jaw. "By you?" he squawked.

"Yes. By me."

"Now that's life with a capital L," said Bruno.

"She wants to be a single mother. She's a beautiful woman in all ways. She nearly drove me crazy until I decided last week to cut my losses and leave her to it."

"You can't do that. It's not moral."

"She won't marry me," Slade emphasised in exasperation. "Harassment isn't moral either."

"Maybe I should take a run out to Halifax and talk some sense into her," Bruno said with a gleam in his eye that Slade had learned to distrust over the years. "My best friend isn't good enough for her? Huh!"

"You do that and you'll never get in a squash court with me again," Slade said, steely-eyed.

"Then you'd better hike yourself back down there. Fast. Time's running out. You've only got three months to change this broad's mind."

"Don't call her that!"

Bruno bent to pick up his racquet and lobbed a high serve that inscribed a graceful curve in the air. Slade reached it in two long strides and hooked the ball into another slow-drifting lob that took Bruno by surprise. With a whoop of frustration Bruno lunged for it and missed. Slade laughed. "My serve."

Bruno tossed the ball his way. "Boy or girl?"

The ball slipped through Slade's fingers. "Boy," he said, and heard how his voice had thickened with emotion.

Bruno shot him a sharp glance. "Does she hate your guts? Is she in love with someone else?"

Slade shook his head. "She's divorced. She doesn't talk much about the husband, but I figure if I ever met him I'd punch him out first and make conversation afterwards." Not even to Bruno would he disclose how Cory had wept in his arms the first time they'd made love.

"Hmm. You want your son born illegitimate?"

Banging his racquet rhythmically against the wall, Slade said, "Not particularly. But I struck a bargain with her back in the spring."

"Negotiate. Compromise. Woo her with wine and roses. Seduce her on satin sheets. But don't just walk away from her, man. You'll regret that for the rest of your life."

"Regret with a capital R?" Slade riposted. "I hear you, Bruno. But I've got to think about it."

"No, you don't, my friend. You think too much. You've got to act." Bruno swished his racquet through the air. "Your serve."

Bruno won the set by a considerable margin, and Slade would have been the first to admit that his concentration was way off. He showered and walked back to work through the September sunshine.

Life continued, and because of what Bruno had said Slade slowly began to realize how narrow a life it was: life with a small l indeed. His work was interesting and challenging. But no one in Toronto argued with him like Cory, or made him laugh like Cory, or filled him with lust like Cory. No one touched his heart as she had, he thought with painful truth one evening in October when he'd come home to an empty apartment after yet one more movie.

What was she doing right now? Was she missing him? Or was she calmly going about her business, with no room in her life for him?

She had room in her life for his son.

He could have phoned her. He didn't. He could have written. He didn't do that either. But—something new for him—he started visiting Bruno and Serena on weekends so that he could play with their two children. This was not without pain, because Tina had just turned three; but as the weeks went by Slade found himself looking forward to Sunday afternoons, and scouting the toy shops for parts for Paolo's model railway and for paints and markers for Tina, who was, he was convinced, a budding artist.

He was having fun, he realized; he was also healing himself. In a strange way he felt closer to Rebecca now than he had for over two years.

Perhaps the very beginning of this process had been the evening in Cory's living room when he'd told her about the accident. He could admit this now, whereas he wouldn't have a month ago.

After one abortive attempt he discovered that he had no interest whatsoever in dating anyone but Cory.

Early one November morning he took the subway so that he could look at a potential building site without getting snarled up in the traffic. As he jogged up the stairs to get back on the street, he found himself behind a heavily pregnant young woman; she wasn't the first pregnant woman he'd seen in the last few months, and he'd learned to expect the soreness around his heart each time this happened.

She was leaning on the arm of a young man in jeans, whose denim jacket wasn't thick enough for the morning chill; he looked about nineteen to Slade. There was solicitude in the way he bent his head to her, and when she giggled at something he said Slade saw that her profile was as sweetly sculpted as the petals of a flower. He hung behind them, and when they reached the top of the steps he watched as they kissed each other goodbye.

"You call me if anythin' happens," the young man said.

"I will, Johnny. Don't you go worryin', now. Hope the job goes OK."

She turned right and he went left. As Slade walked out into the pale sunlight, the young man turned to wave, having reached the corner. Slade pushed his way to the inside edge of the sidewalk, his thoughts clothed in a painful clarity. He's looking after his own as best he can, that kid, he thought. Years younger than me and heaven knows what kind of a job he's got and he's doing his best.

A lot more than he, Slade, was doing.

Here he was in Toronto, while Cory was in Halifax. How could he support her that way? Help her out from day to day? Be with her when she needed him?

With the force of a truck slamming into him he thought, The reason I want to be with Cory is because I love her.

This time I mean it. Every word of it. I'm in love with her.

Which has nothing whatsoever to do with the baby.

The occasional passerby gave Slade a curious look. But otherwise he might as well have been alone on the sidewalk. It was a strange place, he thought as a motorbike and half a dozen taxis roared by, to discover that he was truly healed. That, finally, he had gained the insight to know what he wanted and the courage to fight for it. That he was capable of love again.

It's Cory I want. It's Cory I love.

I've got to get out of here and tell her. Fast.

It was a week before Slade boarded an aircraft for Halifax.

His first impulse had been to fly there that very day. But then, despite Bruno's injunction against it, he'd started to think. He loved Cory and—an obvious conjunction—he wanted to marry her. But Cory was dead set against marriage. The best thing for him to do was move to the Halifax office for the next few weeks. That way he could follow Bruno's advice and woo her, with or without the roses. Take his time. Not rush her. Let her get used to the idea that he loved her.

He asked Mrs. Minglewood to rent him a suite in a building especially for business executives who were making prolonged stays. He worked like a demon organizing his various projects before he left, thankful for the wonders of fax, modems and conference calls that would allow him to work as easily in Halifax as in Toronto. And all the while he felt like a million dollars.

He was back on track. He knew what he wanted. And he was in love. He fantasized about holding Cory in his arms again; standing in a church at her side and repeating the age-old vows of marriage; being with her when the baby was born. In each of these fantasies she was smiling at him, as happy to be with him as he was to be with her.

She might not fall into his arms right away; Slade wasn't so sanguine as to think that she would. But he was sure that if he strategized and kept his head she'd come around.

He arrived in Halifax late in the day. By the time he'd unpacked and had a quick meal it was mid-evening. Taking a deep breath, aware of his quickening heartbeat, he picked up the phone and dialed Cory's number.

After three rings the answering machine clicked on. It wasn't part of his strategy to announce his arrival on an answering machine. He banged down the receiver, picked up the newspaper and found a movie listed that he hadn't seen. He could walk up the street and go to the late show. He'd phone Cory tomorrow morning.

He'd have to phone his mother as well. He had no idea how he was going to explain his stay in Halifax to Lavinia.

The trees were bare of leaves and there was a chill to the wind. Slade zipped up his leather jacket, putting his hands in his pockets. While his hands might be cold, inwardly he was warmed by the knowledge that Cory was somewhere in this same city and that he'd committed himself to her in a way that felt totally right. He'd come to his senses. Finally.

He entered the mall where the movie theaters were located and went down a level on the escalator, his eyes flicking over the billboard. Then he stood in line to buy his ticket. Customers were straggling up the steps from the early shows; he showed his ticket to the attendant and went downstairs, where the air was redolent with the smell of buttered popcorn.

The doors swung open in the nearest theater. While he waited to get some popcorn, Slade idly watched the people come out; he liked watching their faces to see how the movie had affected them. The crowd thinned, until the last people emerged. Among them was Cory, a black-haired woman at her side.

Slade's heart did a leap worthy of a kangaroo. Behind him the girl at the counter said, "Sir? What can I get you? Excuse me, sir. . . ?"

He turned around, muttered, "Sorry, changed my mind," and lunged out of the line-up. Cory hadn't seen him. Dodging through the crowd, he caught up with her at the bottom of the steps. "Cory?" he said urgently.

Cory made a frantic grab for Sue's wrist. She'd know that voice anywhere, she thought, panic-stricken, and looked around.

It was Slade. As always he looked bigger than she remembered him. Bigger and better, she thought wildly. His dark hair was tousled, his gray eyes smiling at her as though the sun had just come up. She said faintly, "Hello, Slade."

His whole face was smiling now. Giving her a quick, comprehensive once-over, he said. "You look wonderful! How are you feeling?" Then he rested his hands on her shoulders and kissed her full on the mouth.

Briefly she felt the warmth of his cheek, the sureness of his lips moving against hers; then, all too soon, he released her. She wanted to grab him by the collar of his leather jacket and pull his face down to hers and kiss him as if there were no tomorrow. She jabbered, "This is Sue, my best friend."

Slade held out his hand. "Slade Redden," he said.

Sue's eyes widened. She gave him a speculative look, her greeting less than warm. Of course, thought Slade. Ralph would have told Sue after the symphony concert that a man called Slade Redden was the father of Cory's child; even though she wasn't quite prepared to be openly rude to him, she was being as protective of Cory as Bruno, in his way, was of Slade. He said, "I've moved to Halifax for a while; I'm staying at the Bronston Inn."

"Moved here?" Cory gasped, her face blank with shock.

"Yes, I arrived this afternoon," he said, and watched her face as disbelief battled with incipient fury. Including Sue in his smile, he added, "Let me buy you both a coffee—I noticed a little dessert place as I came in."

"How long are you staying in Halifax?" Sue demanded.

"Well into the new year."

"I see," said Sue.

He'd be here when the baby was born; that was what he meant, Cory thought, feeling her temper rise another notch. Then she heard Sue say, "I'd love a herbal tea, and Ralph's home with the children so I don't have to hurry home. OK, Cory?"

No, thought Cory, it's not OK.

Taking her silence for consent, Slade put a hand under her elbow. Cory felt the contact shudder through her body. Her coat no longer closed around her waist; despite her pretty green dress and the matching ribbon holding her hair back, she felt large, cumbersome and awkward. Not to mention furious. Furious with her best friend. Furious with the father of her child. Who seemed to think that he could jet back and forth between Halifax and Toronto any time he pleased, dropping her dead in September, then kissing her with devastating intimacy in November. Just as if two months were five minutes.

The first chance she got she'd set him straight. In no uncertain terms.

Wishing she could wake up and find out that this was a movie, Cory marched up the stairs between the pair of them as if she were a prisoner under escort.

The café was charmingly decorated, and there was a table for three in the corner. The menu featured mouth-watering cheesecakes and truffles; as the waitress came to take their orders, Cory said grumpily, "Chamomile tea, please."

"No dessert?" Slade said, raising his brows.

"I'm only allowed to put on three more pounds."

"You can have a bite of my lemon chiffon pie," Sue said, and once Slade had ordered pushed back her chair. "I'm going to the washroom; I'll be back in a minute. Don't eat all my pie, Cory."

As soon as she was out of earshot, Slade said, "I phoned you as soon as I got in. Will you have dinner with me tomorrow night?"

Unsmiling, Cory said, "You look different."

"I feel different. Cory, how are you—really?"

"The bargain was that you live in Toronto."

"I can't do that any more," he said quietly. "Not if I'm going to be able to look at myself in the mirror first thing in the morning."

"So what are you doing here, Slade?"

"I'm inviting you out for dinner tomorrow night."

"That's not what I mean!"

"Cory, a minute ago I asked you how you were."

"Tired. Healthy. And I can't paint my toenails any more because I can't reach them." Also, she continued silently to herself, when I wake up at three a.m. I often feel frightened and very much alone. But I'm not going to tell you that. No, sir. "You're reneging on the bargain."

"Yes," he said, his gray eyes steady, "I am. As far as I'm concerned, it's outlived its usefulness."

"The answer's no. I won't have dinner with you to-morrow night."

"Scared to?"

"Looking after my own interests."

His strategy clearly wasn't working. Slade said levelly, "The baby's our interest—yours and mine... and the waitress is coming with your tea; I'd advise you against telling me where I can go."

Looking as though she was about to explode, Cory gripped her hands together in her nonexistent lap and held her tongue. Then Sue slipped back into her seat, giving Cory's scarlet cheeks a sideways glance. "Have you seen *Rob Roy*, Slade? You have? How did you like it?"

"Sue," he said, "let me ask you just one thing, then I'll talk about every movie I've seen in the last eight months, and that's one heck of a lot of movies. Do you know that I'm the father of Cory's child?"

"Yes. Ralph told me your name back in September."

From between gritted teeth Cory said, "Are you going to announce the paternity of my child to everyone in the city, Slade Redden?"

"No. Only to the ones that matter."

"Your mother?" she flashed.

Trust Cory to go for the jugular, he thought wryly. "I haven't figured that one out yet," he said, and knew it for the weak reply it was.

"Then I'd suggest you give it very careful thought," Cory seethed. She jabbed at the slice of lemon in her tea. "It's been unseasonably warm here the last while—how's the weather been in Toronto?"

"I didn't come all this way to talk about the weather!"

Sue interposed lightly, "Well, I've learned one thing this evening—you're not indifferent to Slade, Cory. Not that I'm surprised; you never were calculating or cold-blooded.''

"No, I leave that to him," Cory said nastily.

"Dammit...." Slade flared.

Her voice laden with sarcasm, Cory retorted, "You just happen to go to the movies where you just happen to bump into me—and then you have the gall to try and pick up where you left off two months ago. When you departed without so much as a by-your-leave. Spare me if I'm not convinced.''

Put like that, Slade thought, it didn't sound terribly convincing. But how could he explain about painting a picture of a teddy bear with Tina, or listening to a young man called Johnny outside the Toronto subway? He said forcibly, "Have dinner with me tomorrow night and I'll tell you what's been going on in the meantime. The all-important details.''

"Sure. After you've had twenty-four hours to concoct them.''

Sue suddenly laughed, a rich chuckle of genuine amusement. "You two sound like Ralph and I at our absolute worst.''

Cory frowned at her best friend. "Two against one isn't fair.''

"It's two against two," Sue teased.

"And I'm for you, not against you," Slade added.

"Oh, do shut up, both of you! And give me a bite of pie, Sue. The first thing I'm going to do after this baby's born is devour an entire chocolate cake all by myself. With icing half an inch thick.''

Obligingly Sue changed the subject by offering her opinion of the movie, and they finished their tea. Then Cory pushed back her chair. "I'm sure it's a tactical error on my part to leave you two alone, but I've got to go to the bathroom. One of the many perils of pregnancy.''

Slade watched as she walked away, his heart overflowing with a complicated mix of love and compassion that she should have lost the lithe grace with which she used to move. Sue said abruptly, "You're in love with her."

"Yeah . . . it's taken me all this time to figure that out. I want her to marry me, Sue; that's why I'm here."

"I'm so glad," Sue said, giving him a gamine grin that lit up her face. "Right from the start I've been telling her it's so much easier to bring up children with two parents rather than one. Providing, of course, that both parents want to be involved . . ."

Her pause was an unspoken question. Slade said huskily, "I want to marry Cory for herself; it's got nothing to do with the baby. But I also want to be a father—part of a family."

"I know the odds don't look good at the moment; she's got a real thing against marriage. But you don't look like someone who's going to scare off easy."

"What was Rick like, Sue?"

"She won't talk about him. Not even to me, and I'm her closest friend."

He said quietly, "The first time I made love with her, I learned a lot about Rick and none of it was good."

Spontaneously Sue reached across the table and rested her hand on his. "If there's anything Ralph or I can do to help, just let us know. I'll invite the two of you for dinner on the weekend; how would that be?"

"She might not come if she knows I'm invited."

"Then I won't tell her," said Sue.

As Cory came into sight, Sue calmly removed her hand and signaled for the bill. "Good luck, Slade."

"Thanks," Slade said, and knew he'd made a friend and gained an ally. And as Cory scowled at them both with open suspicion he decided he was going to need every ally he could come up with. His nice little fantasies had been just that: fantasies. Cory was no more interested in marrying him now than she had been eight months ago.

CHAPTER ELEVEN

HAVING phoned ahead, Slade went to see his mother the next morning in the car he'd leased for the duration of his stay. For a man who'd built a flourishing business in times of recession and was known for his decisiveness, he felt singularly inept and had no plan of action whatsoever. He couldn't lie to Lavinia. But he couldn't very well tell her the truth, either.

Her garden looked settled and harmonious, even in November. Cory's work, Slade thought, and rang the doorbell. Lavinia ushered him indoors and hugged him, then, from her gleaming sterling-silver pot, poured coffee into two bone-china cups; Lavinia liked ceremony. She said calmly, "Lovely to see you, dear. Are you here— rather belatedly, I might add—to marry that delightful young woman who designed my garden? The one who's carrying my grandchild?"

Slade choked on his coffee and rattled his cup back on his saucer with scant regard for its fragility. "How did you—?"

"Slade, I might be over seventy, but I'm not in my dotage. I suspected something was up on my birthday when the two of you met in my garden. The night of the symphony clinched it. I have to say I haven't been very happy with the way you've been behaving."

Another characteristic that had stood Slade in good stead in the business world was his ability to bounce back from a shock. "Neither have I," he said. Then, leaning forward, he poured out the story of the bargain and what had transpired since then. "I did it because of Rebecca," he finished. "But I don't need to be like that any more. I want to marry her, Mum."

Lavinia, who rarely cried, had tears in her eyes. "I was so worried you'd carry the burden of that dreadful accident for the rest of your life, Slade. I'd be delighted to have Cory for a daughter-in-law."

"The baby's a boy," Slade said. "Due at the end of December. But Cory doesn't want to get married. To me or anyone else. She's divorced and her first husband put her off marriage."

"Humph!" said Lavinia. "She certainly didn't look indifferent to you either time I saw you together."

Sue had said exactly the same thing. Slade said pungently, "The opposite of indifference isn't necessarily love."

"The woman who created my garden doesn't have a mean bone in her body," Lavinia declaimed. "I'm sure it will all work out."

Slade wasn't so sure. But when he left Lavinia's after lunch he went looking for Cory. She wasn't at home. He drove to her office and with a quiver of unholy amusement saw that Dillon was the one behind the counter. Dillon stood up when he saw Slade. "Look what the wind blew in," he sneered. "Cory's not here and I'm not going to tell you where to find her."

Slade said in a hard voice, "Let me tell *you* something, Dillon. I'm in love with Cory. I want to marry her. I know it's taken me kind of a long time to figure that out, but that's the way it is. Unfortunately, Cory has consistently refused to marry me—she wants to have this baby on her own. So casting me as the villain of the piece isn't appropriate or accurate." Exasperation getting the better of him, he added, "She won't even have dinner with me, for Pete's sake!"

Dillon's bunched fists relaxed imperceptibly. "You're in love with her? You wouldn't be stringing me a line?"

"Why don't you ask her why she isn't married—to me or anyone else? And while you're about it ask her whose idea it was to get pregnant."

"I might just do that."

"And now are you going to tell me where she is?"

Dillon capitulated with abrupt generosity. "Meetings. With the city. Should be through any time now, and then she'll be heading home. A whole day of bureaucrats isn't Cory's idea of a good time."

"Thanks, Dillon." Slade paused. "Do you have any idea why your boss puts marriage right up there with murder and mayhem?"

"Nope." Dillon grinned. "I put the make on her the first week I worked here. She gave me the cold shoulder— well, it wasn't just cold, it was icy—and yet somehow it's all worked out. We're friends. No sex and we're friends."

For Dillon this was clearly an aberration of nature. Managing not to smile, Slade said, "I'll try her at home. See you, Dillon."

He made a detour to a flower shop on the way to Cory's. The roses recommended by Bruno seemed a bit of a cliché; he settled for a huge spray of tiger lilies whose tawny petals and strong stems appealed to him and drove to her house. Her car was parked in the driveway.

When he rang the doorbell, the door was pulled open instantly. Cory was standing in the hall, still holding her briefcase; she didn't seem surprised to see him. She said ungraciously, "I only just got in and I'm tired. What do you want?"

"I want to give you these," Slade said with his best smile, and passed her the lilies.

She liked them; he could tell. But her flash of pleasure was momentary. "Bribery," she snorted.

"Don't cheapen every gesture I make, Cory! They reminded me of you—passionate and stubborn as hell."

"You do have a way with words."

"There's a word you could try adding to your vocabulary. Yes."

"Yes, you can leave now," she said with a tight smile.

There were bruised shadows under her eyes, and she was leaning against the doorframe, her body tense. Slade said, "On the way down in the plane I read a book about pregnancy—I'll put the flowers in water and I'll give you a back rub and then we'll talk about what happens next."

A back rub sounded the nearest thing to heaven, Cory thought longingly; she was exhausted. And if she could change the corporate mind of the city council committee as she had today she could surely handle anything that came under the rather vague category of "next". Slade added, "I'll even bring you a glass of skim milk."

"No pickled beets? No chocolate cake?"

He glanced at the bouquet in her arms. "Lilies are edible. So I've been told."

Because, beneath all her confusion, Cory was exceedingly happy to see Slade, she said with marked severity, "You'll have to do better than a lily salad with a side order of skim milk if you're going to get even close to the yes word."

He laughed. "Go and change into something more comfortable. You can call me when you're ready."

He took the bouquet from her and headed for the kitchen. As he was locating a vase, he saw that one of the cupboard doors had come off its hinges. He arranged the lilies to his satisfaction, went down to the basement and found a screwdriver and some wood glue, and when Cory came back in the kitchen was just putting the finishing touches to the job. She said drily, "Thank you. One of the taps in the bathroom is leaking; you could fix that too. Oh, yes, and the TV's broken. Why not take a look at that while you're at it?"

"After the back rub."

Her eyes narrowed. "Making yourself indispensable, Slade?"

"Good idea," he drawled. "You look a bit like a tiger lily yourself in that outfit."

"I did a job on Young Avenue and spent my entire commission on it," she said. Young Avenue was one of the most prestigious addresses in town.

She was wearing a wide-skirted caftan whose gold-threaded fabric was a dazzling mix of orange, rust and sunflower-yellow. Slade broke off one of the lilies, tilted Cory's head and carefully threaded the stem through her hair. As his hands brushed her cheek, she muttered, eyes downcast, "You do it every time."

"Do what, Cory?"

How could she possibly explain what she meant? She looked up to find him watching her, an unsettling blend of laughter and tenderness in his face. She was indisputably and irrevocably pregnant by this large, handsome and very sexy man. That she, nearly eight months along, should still find him sexy showed just how sexy he was.

Or how deprived she was. Or both.

"Nothing. Everything. I don't know," she said crossly.

Rather pleased with this response, Slade said, "Why don't we go upstairs? You look like you should be horizontal."

She blurted, "I don't want you to make love to me."

"I'm not here for sex, Cory. It's a lot more complicated than that."

"You know what? You make me feel like thirty going on thirteen," Cory complained, and flounced, as best as she could under the circumstances, up the stairs. She climbed up on the bed and lay down on her side, facing the wall, adding fractiously, "I need to learn to say no, not yes; that's my problem."

"You can practice on every other man who comes along," Slade said agreeably, and eased the caftan up over her hips. She had an apricot silk nightgown on beneath it; he began smoothing the line of her back with his palms, gradually increasing the pressure until the tension left her muscles, and listening for the small sighs of her breathing. Within ten minutes she'd fallen fast asleep.

He took off all his clothes except for his briefs, lay down beside her and pulled the bedspread over them both. As he rested one arm over her belly, he knew with a fierce inner certainty that he'd fight with his life—with a capital L—for this woman and her unborn child.

Cory woke an hour or so later, feeling warm and relaxed and happy; it took a few seconds for her to realize that the source of these feelings was curled into her back, his breath wafting tendrils of hair against her neck. She felt neither frightened nor alone. Not that it was three a.m., she told herself hastily.

She also felt extremely hungry.

"Slade," she said, peering over her shoulder at him, "I haven't eaten for one, let alone two, since eleven o'clock this morning. And I need something more substantial than skim milk."

Smiling at her with his eyes, he clambered over her, lay down facing her and kissed her with single-minded intensity and with all the sweetness of honey. Cory kissed him back—what choice did she have?—her hands cupping the rounded smoothness of his shoulders, then sliding lower to the rough hair on his chest. It had been a long time, she thought dimly—too long, and felt him loose her hair from the gold ribbon at her nape.

Lifting the chestnut strands twined round his fingers to his lips, Slade knew what he wanted to say. He wanted to say, I love you. It was both a simple and a highly complex truth, and he ached to share it with her.

Not yet. It's too soon. Not yet, he told himself.

He said, dropping a kiss on the end of her nose, "Want me to order Chinese food?"

"Sounds heavenly."

They ate chow mein and almond chicken and talked about movies. Slade went home early. The next day he fixed the bathroom tap, took the television to the repair man and for supper made his specialty, chicken teriyaki. On Saturday night they went for dinner at Sue and Ralph's, and on Sunday Slade planted bulbs in Cory's garden—dozens of daffodils and bluebells.

"I'm awfully late with them," Cory said, sorting through a bag of hybrid tulips. "But Dillon's been so busy I've hated to ask him to do it."

Slade trowelled three more holes and scattered some bonemeal in them. "Let's go out tonight," he said. "Put on your best dress and we'll go to that new seafood restaurant everyone's raving about."

The bulbs tumbled from the bag into the holes. "Darn," Cory said. "I'd rather eat home, Slade, if you don't mind." Her voice was almost too casual.

"I do mind," he said, sitting back on his heels.

She said defensively, "I feel like a barrel in my best dress."

"Come off it, Cory—it isn't that you don't want to be seen; it's that you don't want to be seen with me."

"I know a lot of people in this city, Slade Redden. Going to the most popular restaurant in town—why don't we just stand on the rooftop instead and shout at the top of our voices that you're the father of my child?"

He said steadily, "Good question—why don't we?"

"Because I don't want to!"

"I'm not going to go away, Cory."

She had learned by now that the more quietly he spoke, the more she had to beware of what he said. "For me, the bargain's still in place."

"Then we're at an impasse," he said even more softly.

She struggled to her feet, dropping a few more bulbs as she did so. Even though she and Slade had been building up to this ever since he'd arrived, she'd somehow hoped to avoid it. "It's an impasse of your own making," she said agitatedly. "When two people make a bargain, it should take the same two to break it—I don't know how to get that through to you!"

Staring at her, Slade felt his jaw drop; it was as though shutters had suddenly fallen from his eyes, revealing his own behavior to him. "The bargain," he said dazedly, rubbing at his forehead with his fingertips. "I see now why I made it—it's so obvious, yet I never realized it until now." With a real urgency he went on, "I was choosing life, Cory, don't you see? I'd been going around like a zombie for two years, half-dead myself, and then you came along with your crazy idea and I agreed to it. My subconscious knew what it was doing even if my brain didn't. All along I wanted the baby. Right from the start. Of course I did."

Nothing he'd just said made Cory feel any better. On the contrary, his words seemed to clamp themselves around her throat, closing off her breathing, trapping her in the sticky coils of that dreaded word "relationship" like the fly in the web of the spider. "I don't even want to talk about it," she said jaggedly. "As far as I'm concerned the bargain still stands."

"It can't! I—"

"I *hate* arguing like this," she choked. "I'm going inside."

Tamping down an anger that would probably ruin his cause if he gave it free rein, Slade watched her hurry across the grass to the flagstone path that went round the side of the house. His gut was in a turmoil. How *he* hated it when she shut him out!

Then, like a knife ripping through his flesh, he heard Cory scream his name.

Her cry seemed to hang in the air, pulsing as if it were alive. He was on his feet and across the lawn in a flash, dodging the gaps in the flagstone at a hard run. As he came to the end of the rose hedge, he saw her immediately. She'd tripped over the last chunk of stone and had landed on her knees; her back was arched like a bow.

He knelt beside her. "*Cory*—are you all right?"

"My side," she gasped. "It hurts— Oh, Slade, I can't have hurt the baby—not now, not after all this time."

"Of course you haven't," he said, praying desperately that he was right. "I'm going to open the car door; I'll be right back."

Within seconds he was back beside her. "Put your arms around my neck," he ordered. Adrenaline giving him a strength he hadn't known was his, he lifted her in his arms and walked towards his car. "You're heavier than you used to be," he grunted, hoping to make her smile.

But her face was buried in his shoulder and she made no response. As he carefully lowered her into the passenger seat, he saw that her cheeks were drained of color and that her teeth were clamped on her lower lip; he also saw the ugly grazes on her knees. He knew the city well enough by now to know the quickest way to the maternity hospital; he pulled away from the curb, driving no faster than was safe but wasting not one second.

At the emergency entrance Cory was taken in a wheelchair to a curtained bed and her obstetrician was paged on the intercom. Slade stayed by her side, her cold fingers wrapped around his, her nails digging into his thumb. Anxiety and remorse had settled like ice around his heart; if he hadn't forced the issue of the dinner invitation and gone on and on about the baby, this wouldn't have happened. Where the *hell* was the doctor?

As though she had read his mind, Cory whispered, "It wasn't your fault, Slade...my mother always said I should watch my temper."

"I was the one who picked the fight."

She gripped his hand as hard as she could, for even in the midst of a terror unlike any she'd ever known she couldn't allow Slade to blame himself. "No matter what happens, it wasn't your fault," she said tempestuously. "Look at me, Slade!"

As he reluctantly met her gaze, she made a tiny sound of compassion, for his eyes were those of a man in torment. "You've got to believe me," she said with all the force of her will. "I knew that rock was loose; I've been meaning to ask Dillon to fix it for ages."

He said hoarsely, "I'll never forgive myself if—"

"Cory—what've you been up to?"

Dr. Fowler was gruff, female, and sixty years old, and inspired the kind of trust that was often the best medicine. Insensibly Cory relaxed, introducing Slade as a friend then explaining what she'd done, and all the while she kept her grip on Slade's hand.

"Perhaps you could wait outside for a minute, Mr. Redden?" Dr. Fowler said, giving him a speculative look much like Sue's; clearly she hadn't been fooled by Cory calling him a friend.

"He stays," Cory said, the words coming from deep inside her. "If he wants to."

She really wasn't blaming him, Slade thought numbly. Janie's mother, at the funeral, had as much as said that if Slade had been driving there would have been no funeral. But Cory wasn't blaming him. "I'll stay," he said unsteadily.

A few minutes later Dr. Fowler said briskly, "As far as I can tell it's just a pulled muscle, Cory...no need for you to be admitted. But I want you to take the next three or four days off work and I don't want you to be by yourself."

Slade said, "I'll stay with her."

"Good. I'll get a nurse to clean up your knees, and then you can go home. Please take it easy—even though sitting doing nothing isn't your favorite pastime."

With a brisk nod in Slade's general direction she was gone. Cory, as relieved now as earlier she had been terrified, retained her clasp on Slade's hand and realized he was going to be living with her for the next four days.

She hadn't lived with anyone since she'd been married to Rick. "Remind me to remove flagstone paths from my list of gardening options, will you?" she said.

"I don't think you'll need reminding."

The nurse was both swift and gentle. Slade drove Cory home at a more decorous pace and helped her upstairs to her room. Chewing her lip in a way he recognized, she muttered, "I need to lie down. I don't think I can get out of these clothes without some help."

She was wearing dungarees and an oversize T-shirt. Slade undid the metal clasps on the dungarees and slid them down over her hips, then eased the shirt over her head, hearing her gasp with pain as she raised her elbows. She folded her arms over her chest and said in a strangled voice, "My nightgown's under my pillow."

It was the apricot silk one. At a loss to know how to handle this situation, for it was new to him, Slade unclasped her bra and said, "Here, I'll help you with your gown."

She looked as embarrassed as if they'd never made love in this very bed, and as shy as a young girl, and it was this that decided him. Walking round to face her, he very gently rested his palms on her naked, swollen belly and said, "Cory, I want you to know something. I didn't come back to Halifax to try and control your life or to complicate it unnecessarily. I came back because I love you."

"Love me?" she repeated blankly.

His smile was singularly sweet. "I figured it out one morning in the Toronto subway." Raising one hand, he traced the ripe curve of her breast, and felt her beauty as a physical ache. "I'm only sorry it took me so long."

"But—"

"I don't want you to say anything. I just want you to get used to the idea."

Coherent thought, let alone speech, seemed to be beyond her. She shivered a little, muttering, "I'm cold."

The silk of her gown felt as cool as water in his fingers. As he untangled the straps, he said, "One more thing. Every day you grow more beautiful."

He meant it; Cory knew him well enough to know that. Standing a little taller, forgetting that a moment ago she had been cold and paralyzed by shyness, she gave him her most generous smile. "Thank you," she said.

Slade slipped the gown over her head, kissed her and put his arm around her as she got into bed. "Pasta for supper?" he said.

Before she could lose her nerve Cory said in a staccato voice, "You're so different from Rick. By the time he and I split up, I felt such a failure—if I'd been enough for him, he wouldn't have needed other women, right? He was always telling me I wasn't great in bed and I wasn't much to look at...and the sad thing is that I almost ended up believing him." She swallowed. "You don't do that, Slade."

She had never before volunteered so much information about her husband. Slade said gently, "Do you think that the first time we made love I didn't realize what he'd done to you?"

She gaped at him. "You mean it was obvious?"

"It was obvious you didn't want me anywhere near you." He added wryly, "Assuming it wasn't me who totally repulsed you, I could only blame Rick."

"It got so I hated making love with him," she admitted. "But I felt that I had to—we were married, after all."

"Was he violent? Or abusive?"

In a small voice she said, "He married me for my money—it took me a while to realize that, because I was very much in love with him and at first he could do no wrong in my eyes. He's a sculptor, quite a good one...but when I met him he was a student and didn't have two cents to rub together. I had my father's life insurance, and a rather rich and very elderly aunt—so I guess Rick latched onto me for that. Although all along he said he loved me—and maybe he did...how will I ever know? But it was the money he was after."

"Why did you divorce him?" Slade asked, trying hard to keep any emotion out of his voice.

Playing with the edge of the sheet, she muttered, "I couldn't stand him being with other women...how's that for banality? It's such a common story. Such a tawdry story. But it's marked me for life."

"How long since you've seen him?"

"After I found out about Tamara—she would have a name like Tamara, wouldn't she? She couldn't have been a Joan or an Agnes—I tried to kick him out of the apartment. I was paying for it, when all was said and done. But he wouldn't go...Tamara was gorgeous but broke. It was dreadful; everywhere I turned there he was, trying to tell me it was all my fault—I was the one who'd driven him to find Tamara—and Marlene before her and Sherry afterwards. He was like a leech, draining me of my life's blood."

"So what did you do?"

"In the end I left. Stopped paying the bills and got out. And," she added with a wintry smile, "worked myself into the ground at the travel agency."

"And that was when you divorced him?"

"My aunt died first. Surprise, surprise—Rick arrives on my doorstep full of repentance and laden with a bunch of long-stemmed red roses—I've hated them ever since— no thorns and no smell, as artificial as he is. Like an idiot, I let him in. Maybe I still loved him; I don't know. I do know I didn't get married intending to divorce."

She picked at a loose thread in the hem of the sheet. "We had a fight. A huge fight, where I finally said— well, yelled actually—all the things I'd kept bottled up for years, and it began to dawn on him that I wasn't going to let him move back into my life and spend my money just because he'd decided that that was what he wanted to do."

She gulped. "He lost his cool and hit me. I screamed and the little old lady who lived next door came beating on the door with her cane, having roused the university student across the hall who happened to be a champion wrestler." Her grin was rueful. "It was quite a scene. All the elements of comedy without any of the humor."

Slade could imagine it all too well. "I'm glad you had good neighbors," he said flatly.

"Even then, Rick wasn't going to leave. In the end Pete—the wrestler—had to apply the most basic kind of persuasion. I sold the business soon after that and the following autumn moved to Ontario to take the horti- culture course, whereupon Rick married a rich widow from Boston who agreed with his estimation of himself as a genius. End of story."

Slade wasn't at all sure that the story was ended; Cory wouldn't have made the bargain had that been so. But now, he thought, wasn't the time to argue the point; there'd been more than enough emotion in the last couple of hours. He said casually, "You're well rid of him, and we all make mistakes when we're young."

"Not all of us marry our mistakes."

Slade winced. Although, because of Rebecca, he'd never have divorced his wife, in his inner heart he knew how fenced in he'd felt by all of Janie's fears. But it had taken Cory's courage and passion to show him how much had really been missing from his marriage. "Try and sleep for a while," he said, "and I'll ransack your refrigerator."

"I don't know what came over me—I never talk about Rick."

"You just did. Go to sleep, Cory."

Very gingerly Cory adjusted her position on the pillows, listening to Slade's steps diminish down the stairwell. She'd never told Sue about her marriage. So why had she told Slade?

Slade, who said he loved her. Just as Rick had.

CHAPTER TWELVE

THE next three days felt as long as a week to Cory. It came as an unpleasant and startling discovery that a pulled muscle could restrict her actions so drastically; she wasn't used to being inactive. The second unpleasant discovery was that she had very little aptitude for it.

Slade, as far as she could tell and in complete contrast to herself, was having a wonderful time. He'd rerouted emergency business calls to her number, so that when the phone rang she never knew whether it was for him or for her, and otherwise was taking a break from his office. He'd usurped her kitchen, producing meals that were gastronomically interesting and almost always edible, and he'd taken it upon himself to do some long-overdue house repairs.

Cory's area of expertise was outdoors. In consequence there were quite a few of these repairs. He was most considerate, never hammering or sawing if he thought she was resting; he whistled tunelessly as he worked. Everywhere she looked he was putting his mark on her house: a crack filled in the plaster of the dining room, a new doorhandle in the bathroom, a pane replaced in the kitchen window. Gritting her teeth, she knew she had absolutely no grounds for complaint—and knew, too, that it was driving her nuts.

By the morning of the fourth day Cory's pulled muscle was better. She, however, was suffering from an acute case of emotional claustrophobia. She'd forgotten how intensely Rick's refusal to leave had affected her. Now all those old feelings were flooding back, smothering her in their relentless waves. Closed in. Trapped. Frightened. Choose any or all of those descriptions, she thought miserably. They all fit.

Slade wasn't Rick. She knew that. Or at least her head knew it. And part of her present frustration was physical; she was quite prepared to admit that to herself. Slade, without it ever being discussed, was sleeping in the spare bedroom. But for the rest of the time he was constantly underfoot. She couldn't escape the sight of his economical movements, his lean fingers, his incisive gray eyes, until all she wanted to do was jump him.

Jumping, at this stage, was quite impossible.

But it wasn't just sexual abstinence that was the problem. Slade was making no secret of the fact that he was happy to be living in her house. With her. He loved her—so he'd said—and wanted her to get used to that idea.

There had to be more to being in love than getting used to it, Cory thought. You could get used to a pair of ill-fitting shoes. So why should she bother getting used to it? Or to him? When she had no intention of changing the terms of the bargain?

He could leave today, she decided, dragging her brush through her hair in front of the mirror with vicious strength. Dr. Fowler had said four days and they were up. It was time to get back to normal.

She showered and dressed in her dungarees and clumped downstairs, going into the kitchen. It was full of sunlight—the pale sunlight of the approaching solstice; for a moment that was outside time and reason, she saw only the outline of the man standing with his back to her against the light.

He looked like Rick.

Slade had been wondering how best to replace the screen in the little window over the sink; he heard Cory's shocked, indrawn breath and turned around. Her face was as white as the tiles around the sink. "You OK?"

She gripped the edge of the counter and said over-loudly, "For a minute I thought you were Rick."

He stated the obvious. "I'm not."

"The way the light was shining—you looked just like him."

"Cory, I could do without you comparing me to your former husband. The guy was a louse."

"I want you to leave today."

She might as well have thrown ice-water in his face. "Thank you for staying with me, Slade," he said tersely. "Thanks for all your help."

"I am grateful," she said, sticking her chin out. "But I want to be on my own again."

Angrier than he could ever remember being, Slade grated, "So what do you want me to do? Meekly go back to Toronto and forget we ever met?"

"That would be just fine."

"For God's sake, Cory, when are you going to grow up?"

"Oh, sure," she retorted, flushing with temper. "When I won't do what you want me to do, it's because I'm immature. Acting like a kid. We had an agreement, Slade, and you're the one who's not adult enough to stick to it."

"Life doesn't stand still—haven't you learned that yet? In a month's time our son's going to be born. I want you to marry me. I want him to have a proper father."

She winced. "I've already told you I won't marry you."

"Quit looking at me as though I've suddenly turned into the Loch Ness monster," he rasped. "Seeing that you're eight months pregnant, there's a certain logic to a proposal of marriage, wouldn't you say?"

"I will not marry you!"

Struggling for calmness, Slade said, "Don't you think it's time you started to figure out all the implications of what you're saying? There are three people involved here, not just you. And one of them is our son."

"You remember the contract we drew up for the two sites?" Cory retorted. "I should have drawn up another one for our agreement. Instead I trusted your word. Big mistake."

Only the sure knowledge that he was fighting for his life enabled Slade to keep his temper. "I've changed since then. I want to live with you, Cory. For the rest of my days."

"No," she said in a stony voice.

Abruptly Slade turned around, banging his fists on the rim of the sink and staring blindly into the peaceful, sunlit garden. "I'm doing this all wrong," he said.

"There's no right way to do it."

Slowly he turned back. He'd once seen a muskrat caught in a trap, and the animal had stared at him with the same blaze of fear and defiance that he now saw on Cory's face. His anger collapsed. He crossed the floor, took her face in his hands, and said, "I love you—I told you that. The kind of love that's going to last forever, the kind that wants intimacy and commitment." He glanced down. "And a family. How could I not want to marry you, Cory?"

She jerked her head back. "Rick wanted me for my money. You want me for my child. There's not much to choose between you."

"That's a cheap shot!"

"It's true, though, isn't it?"

"No! I was a fool to agree to your terms back in the spring—fool enough to think that a child of mine could come into the world without me loving it or getting involved. I wanted to be safe from another tragedy like Rebecca's death and I thought your bargain would give me that safety. But life doesn't work that way; that's what I've learned over the autumn. Love goes hand in hand with the possibility of loss ... He's not even born, and I love my son." Slade drew a deep breath. "But had he never been conceived I'd still want to marry you."

She had to do this. So why did she find it so incredibly difficult? And feel so incredibly cruel? Striving for the exact truth, Cory said, "I'm not cut out for marriage, Slade—that's what *I've* learned. I wanted Rick to go, to leave me alone, and he wouldn't—every time I turned around he was there. It's been the same the last three days. I was tripping over you all the time, and everywhere I looked there was something belonging to you or something you'd just done to my house—and you won't go either. You won't leave me alone any more than he would. Don't you see?"

"If I stay here, you equate me with Rick," Slade grated, "and if I leave I've lost you. That's not much of a choice."

"I can't help it," she cried. "I don't love you, Slade. I don't love you!"

She meant it, he thought sickly. And that was the bottom line ... she'd never marry him if she didn't love him. Instead she wanted him out of her house and out of her life; she saw no difference between him and a man he, Slade, loathed without ever having met him. In one last effort to get through to her, he said with a desperation he made no attempt to hide, "Until you lay Rick to rest you'll never be able to marry anyone, Cory. Or live with anyone. Why don't you go and see him?"

"Why on earth would I want to do that? I don't love you—for goodness' sake, get that through your head."

It was his heart that couldn't believe it, Slade thought with painful accuracy. "What about the child? Our child?"

Her eyes widened. "You wouldn't try and take him from me...?"

He flinched visibly. "If you think I'm capable of doing that, then there really is no hope... I've got to get out of here; I can't take any more of this."

It was what she'd wanted. What she'd craved. Cory watched him blunder out of the room with none of his usual grace, and the unmasked agony in his gray eyes made her feel horribly guilty and wretchedly unhappy. But it didn't change her mind.

She stayed where she was, propped up against the counter. If this were a movie, we'd have a fade-out now, she thought. Not the sounds of him packing upstairs. Not the anticlimactic necessity of somehow saying goodbye.

Three minutes later Slade thudded down the stairs, carrying his overnight bag. His face set, he said, "I'll let myself out. I probably won't stay around Halifax— you can leave a message on my Toronto number when the baby's born."

Cory tried to think of something to say and failed utterly. He gave her a curt nod and the front door opened and shut. It no longer squeaked on its hinges because Slade had oiled them.

Cory sank down in the nearest chair and rested her head in her hands. He was gone. She was alone, as she'd wanted to be.

Nor would he be back. She was quite sure of that.

She'd achieved her aim.

A week later Cory's business phone rang when she was home for lunch. She picked it up and said crisply, "Haines Landscaping." The phone hadn't rung once all week without her being terrified that it might be Slade. It hadn't been, of course. She had no idea where he was or what he was doing, but she was quite sure he wasn't about to phone her.

"Cory? It's Lavinia Hargreave. How are you, my dear?"

"Very well, thank you," Cory said, hoping she didn't sound as taken aback as she felt. "And you?"

"I've never been overly fond of December—too much enforced jollity for my liking. But other than that I'm in good health. Cory, Dillon has done an excellent job on maintenance but there's something that I feel requires your attention, and I wondered if you could drop in tomorrow afternoon? Or perhaps the next day?"

"Tomorrow would be fine."

"Let's say three-thirty. That way you can have a cup of tea with me."

Promptly at three-thirty on the following day Cory presented herself at Mrs. Hargreave's front door. The unseasonably mild weather had departed; December was making itself felt in biting winds and frosted window-panes. She pulled her coat more tightly around her. At least she didn't have to worry about bumping into Slade, she thought unhappily, and pressed the bell. The garden looked in fine shape to her; perhaps Mrs. Hargreave wanted to add more perennials next spring.

The door opened and Cory stepped inside. Lavinia took her coat and led her into a room Cory hadn't seen before—a cozy little room with a small grate where a wood fire crackled cheerfully. Bookshelves lined three walls. "Sit down, dear, and I'll get the tea," Lavinia said, and sailed out of the room.

Cory, however, loved perusing other people's book-shelves. But as she looked around it was the photographs that caught her eye rather than the neatly arranged paperbacks. Photos of Slade, she thought with an uncomfortable jangling of her nerves.

Slade as a young boy romping with a spaniel in a field. Slade in an academic gown graduating from university. Slade as a bridegroom, with a sweet-faced young woman in an ethereal white gown clinging to his arm and looking up at him adoringly. And finally the one she had subconsciously been dreading: Slade as a father, holding a little girl of perhaps two. Rebecca.

"Of course—you've met my son, haven't you?"

Cory gave a guilty start. That was, she supposed, one way of putting it. "Er—yes."

Lavinia picked up the photo of Slade, Janie and Rebecca. "It was a terrible tragedy when his wife and daughter died in a traffic accident. What made it worse was that Slade blamed himself. He was tied up with a business contract, and so Janie and Rebecca left without him to go to a friend's wedding; he said he'd join them later. He's a very good driver—so he convinced himself that if he'd been at the wheel the accident might not have happened."

The old lady sighed. "We'll never know the truth of that. But the fact remains that Slade rarely even dates now, let alone gets involved with anyone."

Cory stood very still, Rebecca's piquant little features imprinted on her mind. As if it had happened yesterday she could recall the expression on Slade's face when he'd told her about Janie and Rebecca. He'd told her the truth. But not the whole truth. The whole truth—that he had blamed himself—had been too painful for him to share with her. Nor had she asked him for any details. Not one.

And all she'd done since then was push him away.

With a tug at her heartstrings she realized something else. Unbeknownst to his mother, Slade had changed. He'd fallen in love with her, Cory. Despite the past, he'd learned to love again; he'd grown to understand that love and loss were intertwined, and that love, nevertheless, was all-important.

Her brow furrowed. What had he said? Something about the Toronto subway? She'd been too intent on getting him out of her house to even ask him what he'd meant.

How could she have been so insensitive? So blind?

Her thoughts marched on. No wonder Slade had blamed himself when she'd fallen on the flagstone path. In a flood of gratitude she recalled how she'd done her best to convince him it hadn't been his fault. At least she'd done that right.

Although that was all she'd done right.

It didn't seem like very much.

Lavinia said briskly, as if Cory hadn't been standing there staring at the photograph for a full minute in stunned silence, "But then you probably know all this already. About Slade, I mean."

"N-no," Cory muttered. "Not really."

"Ah...I rather thought the two of you had been...what shall I say?...intimate."

Cory's head jerked round and a tide of hot color washed over her cheeks. A pair of shrewd but not unkind gray eyes very like Slade's were fastened on her face. Quite unable to lie, she prevaricated, "I didn't know he blamed himself."

Lavinia pounced. "And would you have cared if you had?"

Slade had already lost one child. And Cory, by sending him away, by refusing to let him have anything to do with her, had banished him from his second child, his unborn son. This fact had been staring her in the face ever since he'd told her about Rebecca, but she'd refused to allow it entry into her consciousness. Wanting nothing more than to put her head down on the nearest shelf and weep, she said through the tightness in her throat, "Yes—I would have cared."

Lavinia nodded to herself. "Let's sit down and have some tea." As Cory levered herself into the nearest arm-chair, Lavinia took the chair on the other side of the fireplace and poured tea into a delicate bone-china cup from a matching teapot. She then offered Cory milk or lemon, and a plate of dainty shortbreads. Pouring her own tea, she said calmly, "I've a confession to make, Cory. I'm doing a quite unconscionable thing this afternoon—I'm interfering in my son's life without his knowledge or consent."

Cory bit into the shortbread, which was absolutely delicious and was no doubt loaded with calories, and waited. The baby was kicking her. No more than she deserved, she decided, and took a sip of tea.

"From the first time I saw the two of you together here at my house I knew something was going on. The meeting at the symphony merely confirmed it. I began to suspect that Slade was the father of your child, and when he arrived here in November I found out that that was indeed the case. I felt he should have married you. He said you didn't want to get married—is that correct?"

Cory planted her feet firmly on the carpet, her fighting spirit coming to her rescue. "Yes, that's correct."

"He came to see me before he left Halifax last week— he looked just as awful as he did those first days after the accident, and that's what made me decide to ask you for tea. I'm sure you think I'm an outrageous old busybody, Cory, but do understand that this is the fate of my grandchild we're discussing—I miss Rebecca still, and it would make me very happy to have a grandson. So tell me, are you in love with someone else?"

"No, I'm not."

"Nor are you in love with my son."

Cory plonked her cup and saucer on the cherrywood table beside her chair, her brain finally going into gear. "Slade didn't tell me you knew he was the father of my child."

"I'm sure he'd consider that an unfair weapon."

"You would be," Cory remarked, "a most formidable mother-in-law."

Lavinia leaned forward. "Let me tell you something else. Janie was a very sweet young woman. But she was timid and retiring, without a scrap of adventure in her. Slade loved her when he married her. As the months went by I watched him rein in his own sense of adventure, his appetite for life, his passion, tailoring himself to fit her world, which was so much more constricted than his.

"Please don't misunderstand me; he never complained and he was heartbreakingly loyal...and, although you might question this, I had the delicacy never to ask what went on between them, in the bedroom or out. He loved Rebecca, of course, with all his heart."

Frozen in her chair, Cory remembered the first time she and Slade had made love, how he'd held back his own needs because she was frightened and reluctant, how he'd eventually brought her to a fulfillment unlike anything she'd ever known. Afterwards he'd told her he'd learned a lot about Rick from making love to her. But she'd never once wondered where or why or how he'd learned such an extraordinary level of self-control.

She'd been too self-centered. Too intent on her own agenda.

I want to make love with him again, she thought. I want to meet him passion for passion, risk for risk. To give as much as I've received. To free him from the past.

"Cory, are you all right?"

Cory gripped the arms of the chair and, her words spilling over themselves, narrated for the second time the story of her marriage and the scars it had left on her soul. "Slade said he thought I needed to see Rick again," she finished. "But I truly don't see what that would accomplish."

"A sculptor?" Lavinia murmured. "What did you say his last name was? Should I have heard of him?"

"Rick Dempsey," Cory said absently. "He's in New York now, as far as I know." She went on rapidly, "Last week... it was too much pressure, Mrs. Hargreave—"

"Lavinia, please."

"I'm due in four weeks and to marry Slade when I felt so closed in—I couldn't do it." She bit her lip. "I couldn't bear to make a second mistake."

In a neutral voice Lavinia repeated herself. "You don't love Slade."

"Love?" Cory said wildly. "I loved Rick and he said he loved me, and look what happened. Slade says he loves me—but how can I trust that?"

"You have to trust yourself first."

Feeling as though something very profound had just been said, Cory whispered, "I suppose you're right."

"I'll be honest, Cory—one reason I invited you here this afternoon was to see for myself what was going on. I like you. I have from the first moment we met. You're capable and fun-loving, and anyone who plays squash and runs her own business is, in my humble opinion, a taker of risks. I'd very much like to have you as my daughter-in-law. But if that's not to be—and it's quite clear to me that I can't make that happen if one or the other of you doesn't want it to happen—I do hope that you'll allow me to play at least a small part in the life of your son."

Cory blinked back tears. "I'd like that," she said.

"Have another shortbread. And can I pour you more tea?"

Cory tilted her chin in a way Slade would have recognized. "I'll be honest too, Lavinia. The thought of never seeing Slade again hurts terribly. But I don't know yet how—how to be with him. I don't know how else to put it. Although I don't suppose it makes much sense."

"It does to me. But if Slade loves you—really loves you—I don't expect he was open to the sweet voice of reason."

"I don't think I spoke with the sweet voice of reason," Cory said with a sly grin.

Lavinia laughed and put another log on the fire. "I love this room; I'm sure I'll be in here a lot through the winter. The weather's certainly taken a turn for the worse the last few days, hasn't it?"

The subject of Slade was closed, and for once Cory was glad to talk about the weather. Half an hour later she got up to leave. At the door Lavinia kissed her on the cheek and said, "Do let me know if there's anything I can do for you. And please put me on your list of people to notify when the baby's born."

"I will," said Cory. "And thank you, Lavinia—you have no idea how dreadful I felt about deceiving you at the symphony."

"You're welcome," said Lavinia, and watched as Cory drove away. She then went indoors, picked up the telephone and dialed the number of an old friend in New York who always kept his ear close to the ground in matters of artistic endeavor.

CHAPTER THIRTEEN

ANOTHER week passed. Cory walked more slowly, left Dillon in charge of the office, and washed her collection of baby clothes and cloth diapers, arranging them with loving care in the nursery. She didn't hear from Slade. Neither did she try to get in touch with him. But she thought about him a lot, fitting into her picture of him all the information she had gleaned from Lavinia.

I'll have the baby first, she thought. Then I'll figure out what I'm going to do about Slade. One thing at a time.

Sue invited her for lunch the next week. Glad to get out of the house, Cory accepted with pleasure and took a taxi because she barely fit behind the wheel of her little car. Sue had already fed the children; Jason was asleep and Amy was playing on the kitchen floor with a collection of her mother's muffin tins and wooden spoons. "Don't bother getting a lot of expensive toys," Sue advised. "It's a waste of money."

She drained the fettuccini and added a creamy basil sauce. "I wasn't going to mention this until after we'd eaten...but have you seen today's paper?" As Cory shook her head, Sue said, "Check out the entertainment section."

Cory flipped through the newspaper and opened it at the listings of movies and concerts. As she turned to the second page she gave an audible gasp. There was a black and white photograph in the center of the page. The man was Rick.

Bewildered, she read the caption, the details slowly sinking in. Rick Dempsey was having a show of some of his smaller works on Saturday in one of the downtown hotels. The public was invited to attend. The sculptor would be present from one until five. Refreshments served.

The paper rattled because her hands were unsteady. "Well," she said inadequately, "I suppose just before Christmas is a good time to have a show."

With unnecessary vigor Sue tossed the salad with a homemade raspberry vinaigrette. "Is that all you've got to say? Do you want me to come with you?"

"I'm not going!"

"Of course you're going. You told me Slade said you needed to see him again. Rick, I mean." Sue grinned. "Sorry, slight mix-up of pronouns there."

"If pronouns are all you've got to worry about, you're doing just fine," Cory said tartly. "Thank you for warning me. I'll know to stay well clear of the hotel that day."

Sue put her hands on her hips. "Cory, there are times I wonder about you! I love my husband dearly but I'm not blind—Slade Redden is a gorgeous, sexy man who also happens to be that rarity—a good man. With money, no less. What more can you ask? But you're going to go round for the rest of your days with that—that *sculptor* dragging from your neck worse than any albatross, and you'll end up a bitter old woman because at some level I'm darn sure you know you're blowing it." She waved the salad servers in the air. "I'll pick you up at one-thirty on Saturday. And don't argue."

Cory snorted. "And what happens if I decide when I see Rick that I'm still in love with him?"

"Stone-cold sober and you're talking gibberish," Sue said sweetly. "Amazing."

"Sue, I don't want to see him!"

"Of course you don't. Apart from anything else, the last time you saw him he belted you one. But I agree with Slade. You need to see Rick again."

About to say a very rude word, Cory noticed that Amy had stopped banging the muffin tins and was listening, big-eyed. She contented herself with announcing, "You should have gone in for psychology, not motherhood."

"I'm not so sure that they're not the same thing." Sue smiled. "Wear that green dress; you look super in it."

Cory looked down at herself. "And what do I tell him when he asks me where my husband is?"

"Tell him he put you off marriage for life. It's the truth, isn't it? Here, have some parmesan."

Cory sprinkled the pasta with cheese and helped herself to salad; salad wasn't fattening. "This last month feels like it's nine months long," she said.

"I know the feeling!" Sue chattered on and to Cory's relief didn't mention Rick or Slade again. But as Cory was going out the door to get her taxi Sue called, "One-thirty Saturday, Cory—don't forget."

As if I'm likely to, Cory thought, and walked heavily down the path. I might not forget. But I definitely might change my mind.

Why should I take Slade's advice? I don't love him, she thought irritably as she eased herself into the back seat of the taxi.

I wonder how he is? I wonder where he is? I wonder if he's thinking about me?

Slade, at that precise moment, wasn't thinking about Cory so much as trying to ignore the dull ache he carried with him everywhere and which sapped his energy until he felt sixty-four, not thirty-four: the reason, he thought, swiping at the ball and missing, why he wasn't even going to be a factor in this game.

"My serve," Bruno said with none of his usual ebullience when he won a rally. He then proceeded to win the point and the game.

They switched sides and began a new game. Slade lost five points in a row. Bruno banged his racquet against the wall and roared, "Slade, ole buddy, will you wake up? It's not like you to present me with the game on a silver platter. It's not like you to give up, either. I curse the day you met that woman. Cory whatever-her-name-is."

"No more than I do," Slade snarled back.

"Kidnap her. Buy the house next door to her. Adopt twins so you won't have the time to think about her. Put an ad in the *Star* saying you want a new woman. But for God's sake do *something*!"

"Back off," Slade said in an ugly voice.

"OK, OK, so forget the twins. But do me a favor. Hike yourself back to Halifax and have it out with her. Or get her out of your mind. One or the other. But quit crawling around like a whipped dog—it's getting to me."

That, Slade thought, was an understatement. Bruno angry was a sight to behold; even his beard seemed to bristle. "Whipped dog?" he repeated, not caring for the phrase one little bit.

"If you don't like that simile, let's try another one. A ball team on a losing streak. A boxer who's been clocked once too often. Or a guy who can't even be bothered to give his best friend a decent game of squash. You get my drift?"

"Yeah," said Slade, "I get it. Your serve."

Bruno sliced the ball at the cut line with all of his not inconsiderable strength. As though it were happening in slow motion Slade saw the ball coming straight towards him. It was a tricky return, one that, if he muffed it, would be no disgrace. With sudden fierce purpose he shifted his feet and drove the ball low into his corner.

By a miracle of logistics and aggression Bruno returned it, and the rally was on. Shot after shot was hit and returned, both men playing as if inspired. Slade ousted Bruno from the T with a wicked backshot and dug in his heels, determined to hold onto it. Three more shots later he won the serve.

Panting, swiping the sweat from his forehead, he said, "You're dead right—I had given up. Came flying back to Toronto like a—"

"Whipped dog," Bruno supplied with a grin.

"Not far wrong, I guess. I'm in Montreal the next few days. But after that things are slowing down—the pre-Christmas slump. I reckon I'll book myself a flight back to Halifax and—as you so eloquently put it—have it out with her."

He rubbed his wet palm down his shorts. Maybe Cory still wouldn't have anything to do with him. Maybe she'd never be his wife. But—somehow—he was going to be a father for his son. A real father. Unlike his own.

She might not want to marry him. But he was damned if she was going to do him out of fatherhood too.

He tossed the ball in the air and took his stance for the serve. He won the game by a score of nine to five.

On the Saturday morning of Rick's show Sue phoned Cory. "You won't believe this," she wailed. "Ralph's got held up in St. John so he's not back until tonight. And there's not a sitter to be had in this entire city; they're all out Christmas shopping. So I can't go with you this afternoon...but you'll still go, won't you?"

"They're forecasting snow."

"It's not supposed to start until this evening. Just in time for Ralph to get stuck at the airport," she added gloomily. "Do go, Cory."

Cory made a noncommittal noise and asked about Jason's new tooth. When she'd put down the phone she wandered into the kitchen. Sue couldn't go with her; they were issuing a heavy snowfall warning; she'd woken up with a dull backache. All good reasons to light a fire in the living room and stay home.

She prowled around restlessly, rubbing at the small of her back with one hand. What good would it do to see Rick after all these years? She'd grown to hate the way he made her feel—so closed in, so much a failure as a woman. Why expose herself to feeling that way again? She'd be crazy to go.

At noon she made herself a sandwich, which she ate with little appetite. At five to one she went upstairs to her bedroom, took out her green dress and stared at it as though it could solve her dilemma.

It was a pretty dress. It suited her.

Slade thought she needed to see Rick again. So did Sue. The only one who doesn't is me, thought Cory.

But Lavinia had called her a risk-taker. Janie had been timid and retiring, had lived what Lavinia called a constricted life. Was that what she, Cory, would be choosing if she stayed home this afternoon? The coward's way out?

What if she never saw Slade again?

Never seemed altogether too long.

She scrabbled in her jewel case for the jade earrings that went with the dress and with some difficulty unearthed her new leather boots from the back of the closet. She dressed hurriedly, trying not to think, and slapped on rather more makeup than was her custom. Her hair, for once, did exactly what she wanted it to do, looping very elegantly on her crown, with some becoming wisps around her face.

Head high, she looked at herself in the mirror, and rather to her surprise saw a bloomingly beautiful young woman with huge brown eyes and a proud bearing.

Go for it, Cory, she told herself, and went downstairs to call a cab.

She arrived at the show too late for the opening speeches; there was a sizable crowd, standing in knots round the various sculptures. Cory saw Rick instantly and in instinctive and primitive fear wanted to turn tail and run.

She shouldn't have come.

Rick was standing at the far side of the high-ceilinged room talking to the president of one of the local universities. Cory took a deep breath, walked further into the room and began working her way towards him, making a gallant attempt to look at the sculptures as she did so. Very little penetrated her consciousness other than the fact that she neither liked nor understood them.

Twenty minutes later, her back throbbing from standing so long, she was within ten feet of him. The small group of people who had been talking to him broke away, and she seized her opportunity. She said clearly, "Hello, Rick."

She saw him start, watched him turn to face her, his eyes glazed with shock. He blinked as he saw her condition. "Cory," he said. "My God, Cory."

Then, like a lamp, he switched on the smile that, all those years ago, had never failed to charm her. As though she were standing by a train track watching the coaches pass one by one, Cory's thoughts followed in procession, one after the other. He's not nearly as tall as I remember him. Or as handsome. Why didn't I ever see how petulant his mouth is? And his eyes are like little pieces of glass—that cold, pale blue that gives nothing away.

He was also, she noticed with immoderate satisfaction, starting to go bald. He wouldn't like that at all.

"Congratulations on your show," she said smoothly.

"Do you live here?" She nodded. "And you've married again?"

"No," she said with a sweet smile, thinking how proud of her Sue would be. "You rather put me off marriage, Rick."

"You've become a very beautiful woman." His lips thinned. "Who's the lucky guy?"

"No one you'd know. And you—are you still married?"

"Not to Coralee...you wouldn't believe how possessive she got; I felt creatively stifled. I married a well-known model just a month ago—you didn't hear about it?"

"I'm rather out of touch with that sort of thing," she said gently. "I do have other things on my mind right now." With a sudden rich laugh that took her by surprise, she added with perfect sincerity, "I wish you happiness, Rick. And now I'd better move on so you can talk to all your fans. Goodbye."

She left him standing with his mouth open. And it *was* goodbye, she thought, heading for the coat rack. Truly goodbye. Why ever had she given him so much power over her life? He held nothing over her now, nor was she the slightest bit afraid of him. But she'd had to see him to discover that.

Slade had been right.

She hunched her shoulders into her coat and tipped the doorman who hailed her a taxi. The sky was a dull, leaden gray, heavy with snow. But Cory barely noticed. She was free—free of the past and of the man whom she'd very nearly allowed to ruin her life.

Her forehead knit, she remembered how Rick had always belittled her, shrinking her down to size so he could control her. In the end she'd rebelled and left him. But ever since then she'd gone on the assumption that marriage meant constriction. Whereas Slade, she thought with a quiver of amusement, had—literally—made her larger. Slade loved her exactly as she was.

Her back was still aching and she was unquestionably still pregnant. But she felt as light as a bird on the wing, as light as the petals of a poppy. She would like, she thought with an inward grin, to go dancing. Too bad it was out of the question.

As she was walking up her front path the first small, lazy flakes of snow were drifting down. It was the kind of snow that meant business; she knew that from long experience. Great, she thought, unlocking the front door. I'm going to light a fire and stay put for the whole weekend. I feel like a new woman. I feel wonderfully, blissfully free.

The door swung shut silently—because Slade had oiled the hinges. Cory found herself staring at them as if somehow they'd conjure up his presence. Throwing her coat over the nearest chair, she went into the kitchen and smoothed her palm over the pane of glass he'd replaced. She then gazed at the new plaster in the dining room as though the blank wall might speak to her. How could she ever have compared her feelings for Slade to those she'd had for Rick?

Slade was nothing like Rick. Slade was solid, whereas Rick was as hollow as his sculptures. Slade loved Cory and their unborn child, whereas Rick was only capable of loving himself.

So why had she sent Slade away?

What a fool she'd been!

Her mind on anything but what she was doing, she laid the fire and touched a match to it. After adjusting the damper, she gazed out the window at what was now a solid sheet of snow. Her brief happiness had vanished; she felt cold inside and out. She'd thrown away her only chance for happiness when she'd told Slade she didn't love him.

She'd made an awful mistake.

She did love Slade. Of course she loved him. Loved him with all her heart, and probably had done from the very first night they'd spent together in the bed upstairs. But she'd been too hung up on the past to recognize it. Too scarred by her marriage and too stubborn to change. And now it was too late. Slade had gone back to Toronto, to a life and friends unknown to her.

She put another log on the fire. She took off her boots and paced up and down on the carpet, her hand pressed to her back. She'd been afraid to go to the hotel and see Rick. But that was nothing compared to the fear that engulfed her now—a cold terror that she might never see Slade again, that her own actions and choices had exiled her from the one man she truly loved.

The wind came up, tossing the branches of the junipers in her garden, the snow whipping like wraiths among the stripped branches of the lilacs and forsythia. Gradually the gray light faded from the sky, until through the white coils of snow the streetlamp glowed fitfully, a gold globe in the gathering darkness. And somehow it was this that broke through the tumult in Cory's breast. She sat down heavily in her rocking chair.

What's wrong with me? she thought. I'm still doing it. I'm still comparing Slade to Rick. I'm going on the assumption that because I sent Slade away and because over two weeks have passed he doesn't love me any more.

He wouldn't change that fast. Not Slade. The kind of love he spoke about was the for ever kind.

She hauled herself to her feet, ignoring an uncomfortable tightening in her belly, and hurried to the phone. Not giving herself time to think, she dialed Slade's Toronto number, the one he had given her for when the baby was born. Her teeth digging into her lower lip, she waited for it to ring.

It rang four times. Then there was a click, a small hiss, and his recorded voice requested her to leave her name and number and the time of her call. Wanting to burst into tears, she waited for the beep then said incoherently, "I saw Rick today and you were right; that's what I needed to do. Slade, I do love you, I just never realized I did, and please don't be angry with me and please come to Halifax as soon as you can." She paused for breath. "Oh. This is Cory. It's Saturday evening. But I'm not going to say goodbye because I never want to say goodbye to you again, only hello and hello and hello for the rest of my life."

She was crying. She put the receiver down and blew her nose and added another log to the fire. Then she went upstairs to change.

The rest of the afternoon passed. She talked to Sue and told her what had happened, and discovered that Ralph had made it home from the airport even though the driving was atrocious. She ate her supper and stared out the window at the blizzard, praying that Slade would come home and listen to his messages.

Was he out on a date? It was, after all, Saturday night.

Impulsively she decided to call Lavinia. Lavinia might know where Slade was. But when she picked up the receiver it gave her nothing but dead silence, and her upstairs phone was the same. The lines were down, she thought uneasily, going downstairs again and drawing the curtains against the swirling snow.

Slade couldn't reach her now.

Ten minutes later the power went off. Cory felt her way into the kitchen and lit some candles then carried them back into the living room. Her backache was worse. Much worse, she realized, gazing into the blue heart of the candle flame. And that tightness, a sensation like being squeezed in a vise, had just happened again.

Contractions, she thought with a jolt. I bet they're contractions.

She wrote down the time on a pad of paper, and forgot everything in her wonderment that the baby she had craved for so long was going to be born. Her son, hers and Slade's. First babies almost always took a long while to arrive and the storm was supposed to blow over by midnight. Maybe by the time Slade got here she'd be a mother.

For three hours the contractions followed no particular pattern. Cory got out her book about pregnancy and with some disappointment decided it was false labor. Maybe she should go to bed. The phone was still out and there was really no reason to stay up.

But then, with dramatic suddenness, the contractions increased in intensity with less time between them. There's nothing false about this, Cory thought, fighting down a panic that if it once got hold of her would reduce her to a gibbering idiot. This is the real thing. I must get next door to my neighbors'.

But when she looked through the window the house next door was in total darkness. Her other neighbor spent the winter in Florida: no help there. I'll go across the street, she thought resolutely. I can't stay here alone.

Moving with painful slowness, gripping the wall as the contractions seized her, she pulled on her coat and managed to stuff her feet into her oldest boots, although doing up the zippers was beyond her. Making sure she had her key, she turned the handle on the door.

The wind rudely thrust the door wide open so that she staggered back, flung against the wall. Snow filled the hall, stinging her cheeks and whitening her coat. Then she felt a new contraction grip her, and, with a whimper of fear and pain, held onto the doorhandle as if her life depended on it.

Eventually the muscles loosened. Straining her eyes, she realized she couldn't even see as far as her gate, let alone across the street. She could fall and no one would know she was there. With grim determination and every bit of her strength she forced the door shut and leaned on it, gasping for breath. Fueled by the same determination, she painstakingly gathered a pile of clean towels and clothes for the baby.

Lots of women had babies on their own; after all, it was a totally natural process. She could do it too. Very carefully she read the relevant pages in her book and all the while every fibre of her being was calling out to Slade. Telling him that she needed him as never before. That she loved him and wanted him here beside her.

That she was desperately and unceasingly sorry for having driven him away.

CHAPTER FOURTEEN

BECAUSE Claude Danvers had invited him for brunch on Sunday, Slade had decided to stay in Montreal over the weekend. He worked on site all day Saturday, took a cab back to his hotel late in the afternoon and headed straight for the fitness room, where he went through his regular routine. Then he took the stairs back to his suite and showered. After wrapping a towel around his waist, he dialed his Toronto number to check for messages.

The third one transfixed him in his chair. It was Cory's voice and for a moment he was sure he was dreaming. "... do love you," she was saying. "... please come to Halifax...hello and hello for the rest of my life..." The words tumbling through his brain, he replayed the tape once and then again.

He wasn't dreaming. It was real. Cory loved him and wanted him with her. For the rest of her life.

With shaking fingers he punched out her number. But after a series of clicks he got only silence on the line. He tried again, and then in frustration got the operator. His French was adequate enough for him to grasp that the phones were down in Halifax because of a blizzard.

He rang the airport. The last plane of the evening was leaving for Halifax in forty-five minutes, although it might have to land in Moncton due to weather conditions. He booked a seat, called a cab and was the last passenger to board the plane. In an agony of impatience he ate what was put in front of him, drank atrocious coffee and sat with his hands white-knuckled as the plane circled Halifax airport for fifteen minutes before deciding to land.

Snow was streaming past the windows. But the pilot made a flawless landing and spontaneously the passengers clapped. Slade had a first-class seat so he was the first one off the plane. He marched along the corridors, wondering if he should try the phone again, and decided he'd rather get there and see Cory in person. It wasn't until he got to the ground-level exit that he fully realized the magnitude of the storm.

"I'll take you in ten minutes," the nearest cabbie yelled. "We'll follow the snowplow into the city."

Slade buttoned his navy overcoat and dived for the front seat of the taxi. "I'll double the fare if you can deliver me to this address," he said, and reeled off Cory's street and number.

"See what we can do," said the cabbie. "First storm of the year always catches everyone by surprise. Just put my snow tires on a couple of days ago. The wife said to me, 'Charlie,' she said, 'last year you didn't put them on until it was too late and you lost a day's pay, so this year you smarten up.' Good thing I listened to her...here comes the plow. Hold onto your hat."

By the time they reached the city Slade felt as though he and Charlie had known each other for years. The main roads had been cleared recently enough that the taxi could cope with the newly drifted snow; but when they came to the turning to the quieter residential neighborhood where Cory lived Charlie pulled up at the curb. "Don't know about this; doesn't look as though it's been plowed at all."

Slade had expected his impatience to lessen the nearer he got to Cory's house, but he now found himself possessed by a raging anxiety to see her, to hold her in his arms and hear her speak those magical words of love to his face. She was all right. Of course she was. It was two weeks before the baby was due. But he still had to see her tonight.

"Maybe I should get out and walk," he said, peering through the windscreen. "It'd only take ten minutes or so."

Then Charlie brightened. "Hold on now; looks like that plow's going just where we want to go."

The flashing gold lights of the plow turned at the corner, Charlie hot on its heels, and it wasn't until then that Slade noticed that the streets were in total darkness, only the flickering of candles illuminating the houses. It was no time for Cory to be alone without phone, heat or lights. Thank God he'd checked his messages.

The two houses on either side of Cory's were as black as the night. But through the banners of snow and the chinks in the curtains he was sure he could see a faint glow of light at Cory's. He took out his wallet, paid twice the fare and added a generous tip, then said, "Look, Charlie, there's probably no need for this, but would you wait here a minute while I make sure she's OK? She's nearly nine months pregnant."

"Sure will," said Charlie, who was the father of four strapping sons.

Slade had to fight the force of the wind to even open the door of the cab. By sheer brute strength he pushed the gate open against a thigh-deep drift, struggled through the snow to the front door, and pushed the doorbell.

No one came. He pushed it again, realized it ran on electricity, and pounded his fist on the wood panels. Through the net curtain he could see that there was indeed light at Cory's. So she had to be home. Surely she wouldn't have gone to bed leaving a candle burning downstairs?

He banged on the door again, and was about to make his way to the back of the house when it occurred to him to try the doorhandle. The door wasn't locked; it flew out of his hand and in a surge of snow he fell into the hall. "Cory!" he yelled. "Where are you?"

Grunting with effort, he slammed the door shut and in the sudden silence heard her gasp, "Slade—is that you?"

He knocked the snow from his boots and headed for the living room. She was lying on the chesterfield. With one quick glance he took in the piled towels, the bowl of water, the baby clothes. In a flash of pure admiration for her courage and her presence of mind, he knew this was the woman he wanted beside him for the rest of his days. He said, "Cory, you've got more guts than any man I know... I've got a cab outside; we'll get you to the hospital in no time."

Her hair was soaked with sweat and even as he watched she started to pant, heavily, like an animal. He grasped her hands and felt her nails bite into his skin and held on with all his strength until the contraction was over. "It had better be no time," she said with a weak grin. "They're only four minutes apart."

The door banged open again and Charlie shouted, "You need any help in there?"

The next few minutes were never very clear in Slade's memory. The two men maneuvered Cory into the back seat of the taxi; Slade struggled back to the house, blew out all the candles and locked the door. Charlie, who had a fine sense of melodrama, slewed round the corner, and with his hand on the horn and his lights flashing drove straight through the intersection. In the first all too brief gap between pains Cory muttered, "I love you, Slade—I love you. I can't believe you're here."

"Thank the pilot, the snowplows and Charlie. I love you too, dearest and most adorable Cory— Here, grab hold." She wrapped her fingers round his wrists, her breath rasping in her throat. "Yell your head off if it helps," Slade urged, knowing he would have given anything he owned to take her pain upon himself.

After what seemed like an interminable time, which tied his stomach in knots, her hands relaxed on his wrists. "I wouldn't want Charlie to end up in the ditch," she muttered.

"Charlie," Slade said, "do you have kids?"

"Yep. Four boys. My wife always sang at the top of her voice when they were being born. Country and western. And you don't worry, lady; I'm not going in any ditches."

So Cory bellowed her way through the next contraction and when it was over said weakly, "That sure helps. Slade, what are we going to call him?"

"What do you want to call him, my darling?"

"I've always liked the name Matthew."

Slade grinned, "Not Xavier Egbert?"

She giggled. "Matthew Slade has a fine ring to it." Then she seized his hands again. "Tell Charlie to hurry."

Moments later Charlie pulled up outside the hospital and ran inside to get a stretcher, and from that point on events blurred in Slade's mind. He did remember being bundled into a green gown. He remembered being impressed by the kindness of the elderly male doctor who had been on call at the beginning of the storm and looked like remaining on call until it was over. He remembered how, at the very end, Cory put a throat-lock on him worthy of Bruno and screamed into his ear, "Tell your son I've had enough! Tell him to hurry up and get born."

Slade's face was jammed against her sweat-slick skin; it was an inappropriate moment to be overcome by a love so earthy and so all-consuming that he knew in his heart he'd never recover from it.

Three minutes later Matthew Slade was born. And Slade was always to remember Cory's expression when the nurse put the baby, with his screwed-up red face, in her arms. Radiant, he supposed, was as close as he could get with words. Although perhaps words had nothing to do with it.

Then Cory looked up. Very gently with her free hand she traced the tears on Slade's cheeks. "I love you," she whispered.

He brought her fingers to his lips. "I love you too. Thank you for our son."

"Silly to cry when I'm so happy, isn't it?" she said, and guided Slade's fingers to the damp fuzz on the baby's head.

Seven weeks later Cory emerged from the office of her doctor, who had been safely home in her bed while Matthew was being born. Dr. Fowler had confirmed what Cory already knew: Cory was in fine health.

She had a plan in mind. A very naughty plan.

She and Slade had been married at the end of December—a quiet wedding, with Sue and Bruno as their attendants and Lavinia in a marvellous red outfit looking extraordinarily pleased with events and with herself. Slade had moved into Cory's house, although they were already discussing buying their own home in the spring, and he had transferred his entire business operation to Halifax. All this had transpired with Dillon's full approval.

Matthew Slade was a delight and a true blessing. Cory loved being a mother.

Slade was a wonderful father.

The only thing wrong with this picture, thought Cory as she walked down the corridor, was that she and Slade hadn't made love for over eight months. Which was an exceedingly long time.

Ever since he'd moved in with her, their enforced abstinence had nearly driven her out of her mind. The effect on him had been the same. She knew it. She'd seen his restraint and the cost to him of that restraint.

And now the time for restraint was over and there was a part of her that felt like the new bride she was—shy and uncertain. But she was also a new bride who had given birth only weeks ago, whose body had, inevitably, changed because of that birth. Would their lovemaking be as wild and passionate as it had been all those months ago? Would Slade still find her beautiful? Desirable?

They had talked a lot in the last few weeks, and she'd learned more about Janie, who had been afraid of so much and whose fears Slade had never been able to allay no matter how stringently he'd tamed himself. She, Cory, felt afraid right now. Silly, but there it was.

Slade doesn't need that, she thought, emerging onto the street, which was edged with February's dirty snow and bitterly cold with the wind from the sea. He doesn't deserve a shrinking violet. He deserves a tiger lily.

In sudden resolution she got in her car and went to the nearest mall that had a lingerie shop. Half an hour later, her coat buttoned to her chin, carrying a plastic bag and a slim paper-wrapped sheath with a flower inside it, she came outside and drove home.

Slade had stayed with the baby. With any luck at all, Matthew would be asleep.

Having parked in the driveway, she undid the paper and took out the lily that it contained. Then, her heart hammering as though she'd just played a game of squash, she ran to the front door, slipped inside and put her shoulder bag, now bulging, inside the closet.

Slade came into the hall. He was wearing jeans and a denim shirt; his hair was still damp from the shower. "Is Matthew asleep?" she asked—she hoped innocently.

"Fast asleep."

Her eyes very bright, she brought the lily from behind her back, held it out to him and said, "Help me off with my coat, would you, Slade?"

He took the flower, gazing into its vivid orange heart. Then he looked up. Cory's hair was loose on her shoulders and her cheeks were flushed from more than the cold; he loved her so much and found her so achingly beautiful that he would have done anything she asked. He put the lily on the nearest chair and walked up to her. "Welcome home, Mrs. Redden," he said, and kissed her with all the pent-up passion of the past eight months.

Heaven, Cory thought dimly; this is heaven. Then she felt him reach for the top button of her green wool coat. Briefly her lashes dropped to her cheeks.

His hands very sure of themselves, Slade undid the buttons one by one and spread the coat apart. Beneath it she was wearing a low-cut lacy black bra, lace-trimmed black bikini briefs and long black stockings. Her cheeks were by now a vivid scarlet.

Feeling laughter gather in his chest, laughter and a most unsettling mix of lust and pure happiness, Slade said, "Would you be trying to seduce me by any chance?"

Her eyes were brimming with a matching laughter. "That's one thing I like about you—you catch on fast."

"I try." He grinned. "What else do you like?"

Cory ran her hand down his chest, past his belt buckle, and still lower, feeling his body's instant response. "You're no slouch in that department either."

"You go right for the essentials, dearest Cory."

With a seductive pout, moving her hips in sinuous and blatant invitation, she said, "I was going to have the lily clenched between my teeth. But it tasted kind of funny."

He laughed out loud. "Cory, Cory...if I'd known, I'd have had flamenco music on full blast. Do you wonder that I love you?"

"Sometimes," she said honestly.

"Never doubt it," he growled, kissing her again just to convince her. "You'd better keep your coat on while I carry you upstairs. Just in case the neighbors are watching."

"We don't need Charlie this time." They had sent Charlie an announcement of the birth, and he had responded with a charming little teddy bear that had pride of place in Matthew's crib.

Slade picked her up and started up the stairs. "You're considerably lighter, I have to admit."

"No grunting and groaning?" she teased.

"That, my darling, comes later."

He put her down by the bed, divested her of her coat and himself of his clothes, and said, a catch in his voice, "We've waited a long time for this."

"Yes," said Cory. She lay down on the bed, pulled him down beside her, and with unpracticed enthusiasm and deep hunger set out to seduce her husband. Not that it was difficult. In fact, it was astonishingly and delightfully easy because Slade's response was, to say the least, flattering, while all she wanted to do was to give of herself from the abundance of her love.

And Slade, even in the midst of a passion beyond his imagining, was able to recognize her generosity, her unbridled caresses and fierce mating for the gifts that they were, and loved her—if possible—all the more.

They fell asleep in each other's arms and woke to the baby's crying. "Why don't I feed him," Cory said with a lazily provocative smile, "and come back to bed?"

Slade stroked the swell of her breast to its tip, and watched her face quiver in response. "Good idea—we've got a lot of time to make up."

"But a lifetime to do it in."

"No reason not to start now," said Slade.

Half an hour later Matthew, dry and fed, went back to sleep; and Cory, wide awake, went back to bed.

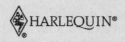

Not The Same Old Story!

 Exciting, glamorous
romance stories that take
readers around the world.

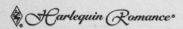 Sparkling, fresh and ten-
der love stories that
bring you pure romance.

 Bold and adventurous—
Temptation is strong women,
bad boys, great sex!

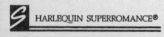 Provocative and realistic
stories that celebrate life
and love.

 Contemporary
fairy tales—where
anything is possible
and where dreams
come true.

 Heart-stopping, suspenseful
adventures that combine the
best of romance and mystery.

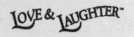 Humorous and romantic stories
that capture the lighter side of
love.

Take 2 bestselling love stories FREE

Plus get a FREE surprise gift!

Special Limited-Time Offer

Mail to Harlequin Reader Service®

3010 Walden Avenue
P.O. Box 1867
Buffalo, N.Y. 14240-1867

YES! Please send me 2 free Harlequin Presents® novels and my free surprise gift. Then send me 6 brand-new novels every month, which I will receive months before they appear in bookstores. Bill me at the low price of $3.12 each plus 25¢ delivery and applicable sales tax, if any*. That's the complete price, and a saving of over 10% off the cover prices—quite a bargain! I understand that accepting the books and gift places me under no obligation ever to buy any books. I can always return a shipment and cancel at any time. Even if I never buy another book from Harlequin, the 2 free books and the surprise gift are mine to keep forever.

106 HEN CH69

Name	(PLEASE PRINT)	
Address	Apt. No.	
City	State	Zip

This offer is limited to one order per household and not valid to present Harlequin Presents® subscribers. *Terms and prices are subject to change without notice. Sales tax applicable in N.Y.

UPRES-98

©1990 Harlequin Enterprises Limited

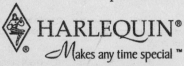